SUGAR
and
SPITE

GAIL D. VILLANUEVA

Scholastic Press / New York

Library of Congress Cataloging-in-Publication Data available

ISBN 978-1-338-63092-3

1 2021

Printed in the U.S.A.   23

First edition, April 2021

Book design by Baily Crawford

To Quackie, our sweet and cheery girl
who gave us so much joy.
To Kubrick, our good boy who saved us
over and over again.
To Shantee, our sassy girl who brought
light into our lives.
And to all the dogs, ducks, cats, turtles, hamsters,
and chickens we've loved before.

We love you still, and miss you every day.

CHAPTER ONE
Mean Claudine

There are two kinds of magic. One happens by chance. For example, your cooking-challenged mom makes an amazing chicken adobo by accidentally dumping the right ingredients in a pot. Or maybe you find yourself having car trouble and a stranger just walks up to help you. Totally random, everyday miracles.

But there's also the kind of magic you intentionally make happen. The kind that some people find hard to believe— it's magic that *can't* be real, but it actually is.

Ever since my parents and I moved to Isla Pag-Ibig from Marikina City in Metro Manila, I've seen more of the intentional magic than the random one.

Because my grandfather, my lolo Sebyo, can do the intentional kind—and so can I.

Well, sort of.

Lolo Sebyo is an arbularyo, a faith healer. He heals

people with prayer, herbal oils, and massage. Sometimes, even with magic—real magic.

I'm Lolo Sebyo's apprentice. And part of being an arbularyo-in-training is running errands for Lolo like buying herbs and groceries from the wet market.

Woof!

My dog, Kidlat, runs to the river before I can stop him. He's like a brown-and-white cannonball splashing into the water by the side of the road.

"Oh, come on!" I groan. I'm tempted to join him. It's a Friday afternoon, and the sun is out—a much-needed break from the usual early-September rains. But the stuff I bought is heavy and I know I should bring it right home. "Lolo's waiting for us. We don't have time for this."

Kidlat stops splashing about. He looks at me with his big brown eyes. I imagine him saying, "You know you want to, Jolina!"

"Okay, you win," I say with a sigh, securing my shopping bag behind a giant rock. I hoist my shorts up and join my dog in the water. Kidlat's begging is totally manipulative. Yet I still fall for it. Every. Single. Time. "Let's go swimming. But just for a bit."

The water is cold on my skin and so clear I can see my toes. Above, the afternoon sun peeks through a canopy of leaves and branches. The rays touch the water's surface, making little specks that look like tiny, dancing fairies of light.

I have to admit Kidlat's right. Taking a dip is a great idea. "You're such a smart boy!"

Kidlat swims beside me. His nose is warm as it nudges my thigh.

"You like this?" I scratch Kidlat on the two brown spots behind his ears. I love him so much. We wouldn't have been able to afford to get a dog of his breed—he's a Jack Russell terrier with a fancy pedigree. But our kind neighbor in Marikina City gave him to me as a gift when I was five.

I'm twelve now, and Kidlat and I are still the best of friends. Our best friendship will last till the end of time.

Kidlat floats on his back in my arms and closes his eyes.

I giggle. "Silly dog."

Mom said there used to be more water flowing through this shallow river. It was so deep, she couldn't walk on the bed the way I'm doing now. But things change.

Like my life. I never expected my family to move away from Marikina City. I close my eyes like Kidlat does. Marikina is an old city. It has a river too, but no way you'd want to swim in it. Mom said someone once had the idea of using janitor fish to clean the dirty water. That plan backfired—the river is not only still dirty, it's also full of janitor fish now.

"Well, well, well. If it isn't little *Joh-lai-nah* Bagayan."

Ugh. Not *her* again.

So much for a nice afternoon swim.

Claudine Dimasalang sits on a giant rock on the riverbank. She's brown but lighter than me and has the high-bridged nose and deep-set eyes I wish I had. Her wavy black hair has bright pink, blue, and purple highlights.

And she *knows* my first name is Jolina. As in, *Joh-lee-na* with a long *e*. We've been attending the same Bible study group since my family moved here three months ago. She's also been making my life miserable since then.

"You not supposed to take a bath there, *little* girl," she says in this bossy voice that grates in my ears. Listening to Claudine is like hearing fingernails scratch a blackboard. It's irritating *and* painful.

She loves to bring up my height, but it's not like Claudine herself is that tall. Sure, I'm a bit on the short side—my homeroom teacher in Marikina always put me up front during the flag ceremony. And admittedly, Claudine is a head taller than me. But calling me a little girl is too much of a stretch, especially when I'm five months older than she is.

"I don't see a sign saying I can't swim here." My jaw clenches. *I mustn't get angry.* It's hard to do whenever Claudine's around. I muster a smile that makes me look like I just swallowed sinamak vinegar. "Other people swim here."

Claudine raises her eyebrows, her lips curved into a smirk.

Okay. I *think* people swim here. I was so sure they

did. But now that Claudine's here, I can't be certain anymore.

I just hate how easily Claudine makes me doubt myself.

"Do you see anyone else here aside from you and your dog?" she sneers, flipping her hair over her shoulder. Claudine's always messing with her hair.

"But no one says I can't." I'm not letting her get the best of me. "In Marikina, we have signs for things we're not supposed to do."

Claudine's sneer turns into a scowl. "You're far from Manila now. You can't bring your disgusting habits here and force them on everyone else."

What is wrong with this girl? "I'm not forcing my habits on anybody—"

"I saw your mother at the resort today."

I grit my teeth but say nothing.

Claudine's family owns the biggest luxury resort in Isla Pag-Ibig—the very same resort where my mother works.

Don't say anything. Don't do anything.

I take a deep breath, then exhale slowly like Mom taught me. She practices a lot of calming exercises. And I really, *really* need to be calm right now.

"Your mother would be so horrified to hear what you've been doing," she says coyly. "What if I tell *my* mother to tell *your* mother—"

"You wouldn't." Well, I hope she wouldn't.

I'm still not sure what I'm doing wrong, but Mom is

a trainee. She doesn't have the privileges of a regular employee yet. Like, they can fire her anytime. And I don't want to give Claudine's mom any reason to.

I have a bad feeling Claudine knows that too.

Claudine flips her hair again. "How would you know?"

I ball my fists. It's getting really, really hard for me not to lash out.

Claudine looks pointedly at my hands. "What are you going to do, use your magic wand on me?"

Ugh! I hate being powerful and so powerless at the same time. I have magic, but I can't use it on this mean girl. It's one of Lolo's rules: *Never use magic to hurt others. We heal people. We don't harm them.*

Besides, I don't have a magic wand. My family's magic doesn't work that way.

"Come on, good boy," I tell Kidlat, looping my arm around his tummy as I wade away from Claudine.

But she's obviously not done with me yet.

"You only have magic because of your family," she spits. "If it were up to me, I wouldn't give it to an untalented nobody like you."

Ouch.

Okay, so . . . I'm not very good at magic. I don't even know why my lolo keeps trying to teach me. Granted, I only started magic lessons a few months ago when we moved here. But every single potion I've tried to brew has so far been nothing but a big glop of failure.

Like I said, Claudine Dimasalang really knows the best way to make me feel like my worst self.

I still keep my mouth shut even as a lump forms in my throat. *Think about Mom. You'll get Mom in trouble if you fight back*, I tell myself over and over again.

"Why can't you just leave me alone?" My voice cracks as I punch my fists into the water.

Kidlat must sense my pain—he licks my cheek. Doggie kisses are nice, but I want Claudine to just go away.

"Don't flatter yourself, *Joh-lai-nah*." Claudine snorts. "You have so much to learn about life here in Isla Pag-Ibig, *dayo*."

Dayo. A visitor. I've been trying to make this island my new home for my family's sake. But there are people who will never accept me. People like Claudine.

I hold Kidlat tighter. His calming presence is the only thing that's stopping me from answering back.

Mom's job. Remember, Mom's job.

"Free advice for you, dayo." Claudine points at the north end of the river, the side where the water flows down from the mountain. "You never swim in the downstream path of a bathing carabao."

My eyes follow the direction where she's pointing. Claudine's right—there *is* a bathing water buffalo. An image of it pooping flashes in my head, and I immediately splash back to the riverbank.

Gross!

Claudine laughs. "See you around, *Joh-lai-nah*."

So much for a peaceful afternoon swim.

I don't know how long I can put up with this. But my parents have enough to worry about already—we can't afford getting Mom fired from her job too.

I wish I could use magic on Claudine. I wish Lolo could channel his powers and transform her into a water buffalo. Or at the least, I'm sure there's a potion to turn her into a nice person or something. But Lolo would never use magic with bad intentions.

One day, Claudine will get what she deserves. Life will find a way.

Well, I hope it will. Because it would be too unfair for Claudine to keep getting away with being mean to everyone who's not as rich as she is.

CHAPTER TWO
The Mango Tree

Isla Pag-Ibig is a weird-shaped island. It's very tiny. You probably won't see it on the Philippine map. But if you use an online map where you can zoom in on stuff, you'll notice that it actually resembles a heart tilting to the right. The indent of the heart, which faces the Philippine Sea, is owned by Claudine's family. It's where her mother built their resort on a beautiful white-sand beach.

Lolo Sebyo's home is in Barangay San Pedro. The barangay—the village—is a very small coastal community on the west side of the island. We're far from the town proper, where the island's rich families and businesspeople live. Our beach has dark sand and is full of pebbles. There are sharp corals in the breakwater ten meters from the shore, which cut your feet if you try swimming without sandals or flip-flops.

Later that evening, I hoist myself up on a branch of the

old mango tree in my grandfather's yard. It reaches over Lolo Sebyo's potion lab, sheltering it from the elements with its sturdy, ancient branches. It's a miracle this tree is still standing. Dad says mango trees don't grow roots deep enough to withstand typhoons, except for this one. He thinks the mango tree knows it's protecting something important.

This mango tree is also my favorite place to hang out. The view from it is just amazing. Across the water, the town of Bulusan leaves a perfect outline on the horizon, separating heaven from the sea. The sun turns the sky dark blue and orange just before the stars begin to appear.

"Oof!" I grab a branch to steady myself as Kidlat jumps on the branch next to me. He slathers my face with dog kisses before I can complain. "Okay, okay. You're forgiven."

I look up the mango tree. There's still some fallen fruit on the ground that we weren't able to harvest, but thankfully, mango season's over. Last month, an overly ripe mango nearly fell on my head. If Kidlat hadn't warned me, I would have been knocked out.

"I love you, fur-ball. I don't know what I'd do without you," I tell my dog, hugging him close. Kidlat nuzzles my neck in response. His short fur tickles my skin. I giggle, bringing my phone up behind him. "Let's take a photo."

On cue, Kidlat goes into selfie mode. He tilts his head and widens his eyes.

I hold up my phone and do the same, grinning like the happy girl that I'm not.

Lolo Sebyo always says I have all the features of a Bagayan. High forehead, a flat nose, and big eyes. Dark brown skin. Mom tells me my eyelashes are beautiful, and my black hair is straight and thick, but I don't think anyone but her has ever noticed.

Then again, Mom isn't as dark as me. I may have inherited the Bagayan arbularyo potential, but I also got Dad's dark gums.

Dad says our dark gums are caused by melanin. Bagayans have a lot of melanin. More melanin also means darker skin, which Lolo, Dad, and I have.

Kidlat whines. I look down and find him still keeping up his pose.

"Oh, I'm so sorry!" Giggling, I snap the picture and turn off my phone. Like clockwork, he snaps out of his selfie mode.

"Such a strange dog!" a deep voice says. From my low perch, I find my grandfather leaning on his walking cane and smiling at me. "He understands technology better than I do."

"Lolo!" I exclaim. Kidlat jumps off the tree and goes to greet my grandpa. Lolo Sebyo is recovering well from his stroke earlier this year, but his legs still aren't as strong as they used to be, and I don't want him to lose his balance. I hop down after Kidlat and grab his harness before he can stand on his hind legs to jump on Lolo, but my grandfather just laughs and scratches my dog's ears.

I take Lolo's other hand, touching its back to my forehead. "Mano po—your hand, please."

In response to my sign of respect, Lolo Sebyo draws a cross in the air. "God bless you."

"I bought the stuff you needed, Lolo." I beam at him. "I left it in your lab. Did you see?"

"Oh, yes! Thank you, my Bee," says Lolo Sebyo.

My family calls me "J-Bee," or "Bee," from my full name, Jolina Beatrice. I'm lucky Claudine doesn't know that, or I'd never hear the end of it.

"Bad day?" Lolo Sebyo smiles. It's a small smile, but somehow, it takes away some of my sadness.

How does he know? Lolo really is magical. He may even be able to fix my problem with Claudine, but I can't tell him about her. I don't want him to talk to Claudine's mother and cause problems with Mom's job. Don't get me wrong, Lolo Sebyo wouldn't intentionally do anything to jeopardize Mom's job. But seeing how awful Claudine is, I have a bad feeling her mother might be the same way. The mango doesn't fall far from the tree after all. It just falls right under its branches, or on top of my head.

"Kidlat and I accidentally took a bath in Kaibigan River with a carabao, Lolo," I say, nodding glumly. That's part of the truth, at least.

"That certainly sounds bad." Lolo Sebyo chuckles, ruffling my hair the way he scratched Kidlat's ears.

I pout. I know it sounds silly, but he didn't have to laugh. "I'll always just be a dayo in this island. I'll just be this Manila girl who'll never get the ways of the Islanons."

"I'm sorry, little Bee. I should not have laughed." Lolo Sebyo's expression turns serious. "Coming to a new place is always hard. But you will fit in eventually. Just have a little faith."

I study Lolo Sebyo. The right side of his face is drooping slightly, making him seem older than his late sixties. He's a short, thin man with a huge bald spot in the middle of his head of white hair. Lolo Sebyo has dark gums too, but they're hidden under his dentures. I wonder if there are dentures that would let you keep your teeth but can hide your dark gums. I'd buy one of those, for sure.

"I hope you're right, Lolo," I say, sighing.

I do well in school—great, even. Like, honors kind of well. The public school here is teaching us stuff I already learned last year from the Montessori I went to in Marikina. My classmates are friendly, but I'm not close to any of them.

I guess I'm sending out a "dayo vibe" to my Isla Pag-Ibig classmates. Or, more likely, Claudine must have told them bad things about me. Claudine is homeschooled, but some of my classmates are also in the Bible study group Claudine and I both attend, and she's always chatting with them.

The irony is that despite feeling like an outsider, my family's magic is accepted by everyone in a way it never was in the city. Many of the islanders are my grandfather's customers, after all. Back in the city, I couldn't tell anyone about my family. I was afraid they would mock my grandfather and call him a scammer, since the only "arbularyos" they'd met were the fake ones who ask for odd things like roast chicken and pancit canton as "spirit offerings." Lolo Sebyo *never* asks for anything in return for his magic.

"Come with me, little Bee." Lolo Sebyo dusts dirt off my clothes and tucks a lock of hair behind my ear. "We still have about thirty minutes before the moon arrives. Magic is tricky to use in the moonlight."

I follow Lolo Sebyo to his potion lab with Kidlat trotting behind me. "For what po, Lolo?"

My grandfather gives me a kind smile. "You shall see."

CHAPTER THREE
A Dose of Happiness

Lolo Sebyo's potion lab is like a cross between an apothecary and a library. Well, I've never been to an apothecary, but it's how I imagine it to be. Behind a long wooden table, rows upon rows of multicolored bottles line one side of the room. The other side is full of books. Ancient books. Like, books that are so old, they were around even before the 1896 Philippine Revolution.

I'm not kidding. Lolo Sebyo said our ancestors fled from Pampanga to Isla Pag-Ibig during the Spanish era to escape the church's arbularyo purge. He doesn't know when exactly, but for sure it was way before Filipinos decided they had enough of Spain's oppressive regime.

The Spanish called our family heretics. Which was funny, considering *they* merged Christianity with the magical practices of pre-colonial tribes to make us accept their religion.

Colonizers are weird.

"Are we going to make a potion?" I ask, setting Kidlat down on the floor. He bounces straight for Lolo's books. "But it's Friday night!"

"That is true." Lolo Sebyo nods as he brings out ingredients from the cupboard. "I hope you do not mind having an extra lesson."

"Of course not!" If it were up to me, I'd want arbularyo training every day. But it's not, so I still go to regular school and train on Saturdays. As Lolo says, *Arbularyos need to learn about the world they live in.*

"Good." Lolo Sebyo points at Kidlat, who's sniffing the shelves with great interest. "Don't let him lick my books, little Bee. Those are very, very rare! Can't find them anywhere else on the island. No. These have been in the family since before Spain invaded the Philippines."

Like I said, those books are *old*.

I grab Kidlat from behind. Most dogs might resist being carried like a baby, but not my good boy. He's absolutely still as I carry him away.

"Put your dog down and come over here," says my grandpa, waving me over. "And let the light in. I must finish this today before my patient comes."

Lolo Sebyo likes to call the people who ask for his help "patients." He says that in some places, an arbularyo is called a "witch doctor" instead of a faith healer. So, in some way, he's also a doctor.

I head for the window near the table and open the black

curtains. The glass is covered with thick black paper except for a small hole, where the dusk's remaining sunlight streams in. The ray illuminates a clay pot on a portable stove in the middle of the table. It has a perfectly round bottom and a spread-out rim. A palayok.

Lolo Sebyo lights a blue candle. "Join me in prayer, my Bee."

I clasp my hands together and lean in toward the palayok like Lolo does. He utters the protection chant and I whisper along with him. We ask the Lord to bless our brew.

My grandpa makes the sign of the cross, ending our prayer by telling God that we are offering everything to him. "Ang lahat ng ito ay alay namin sa inyo, Panginoon."

I do the same and reach for the wooden ladle on the table.

"Not this time, my Bee." Lolo's hand covers mine. He gently takes the ladle from me. "You are too emotional at the moment. Even for an experienced arbularyo, it's nearly impossible to balance magic and strong emotions when you're making the brew. But I want you to watch. You will make your own potion tomorrow morning."

My face falls as I take my pen and journal from under the table. See? This is what I was talking about. I'm not a very good arbularyo—which Claudine was nice enough to remind me of. Lolo Sebyo often reminds me to "balance magic and emotions." I've been doing exactly that. I could feel the magic and emotions I let go and hold back are just right. I *know* the balance is spot-on.

But I still can't brew anything correctly. It's almost as if the magic itself doesn't like me. It's my birthright and yet it seems to intentionally not want to work well for me.

Sometimes I really wonder if Lolo Sebyo regrets agreeing to take me on as his apprentice. Or that he thinks I'm a horrible arbularyo but has no choice since Dad doesn't do magic and Lolo needs someone to carry on the family tradition of potion making.

Lolo Sebyo combines all the ingredients in the palayok, dipping the wooden ladle as the mixture turns into a clear blue liquid. "We are making a Dose of Happiness for a patient who needs a little help getting through the weekend. First step is to stir the potion once clockwise, then immediately stir twice counterclockwise."

The liquid turns opaque, like someone poured milk in it. The potion's texture becomes thick and creamy like hot chocolate. But blue.

"Pretty!" I say, taking down notes. I love the color blue. It reminds me of the sea.

My grandfather returns my smile. "Now, very carefully, we will need to keep stirring the potion clockwise as we put in sage and peppermint."

Lolo Sebyo tosses in a small bundle of the dried herbs. The potion hisses and melts the bundle. "Just some more stirring. A little faster, but still with care. Breathe in, breathe out. Here you will let the palayok channel your magic into the potion."

The potion fizzles and hisses, then bluish smoke rises from it. The blue smoke smells like chocolate.

"Ohh!" I close my eyes, savoring the scent, and getting so absorbed in it that I almost forget to write down the last set of Lolo's instructions. "That smells so good!"

"It's done!" Lolo Sebyo turns off the stove and pours the potion into small bottles. "Can you help me make some labels? I will need a dozen for this batch."

"A Dose of Happiness," I mutter as I write the labels. I try to do a good job, forcing my handwriting into something better than my usual chicken scratch–like scrawl. Lolo Sebyo takes the stickers and puts them on the bottles full of blue liquid.

"That sounds like something that could cheer me up. Instant happiness!"

"Not quite." Lolo Sebyo chuckles. "A Dose of Happiness is only a temporary cure for sadness, not meant as an answer to anyone's problems. Quite similar to the medication for mood disorders, except this one addresses more than a person's moods—it soothes the soul as well as the mind."

My eyes land on a framed photograph on Lolo Sebyo's table, the one of his late wife, my lola Toyang. I miss Lola Toyang, but not as much as Lolo Sebyo does. She was the love of his life. He was so sad when her breast cancer suddenly turned for the worse in March. Dad said the stress of seeing her suffer and being powerless to stop it must have caused Lolo's stroke.

I used to think that Lolo Sebyo handled Lola Toyang's death okay because he knew we would be moving in with him here on Isla Pag-Ibig. Or maybe he was just able to prepare better for her inevitable passing. But now that I know what a Dose of Happiness can do to a person . . . it makes me wonder if Lolo Sebyo ever uses his own magic on himself. "Magic can't heal everything, can it?"

"No, it cannot heal everything. Like I said, it's only a temporary fix. True healing must come from within the patient themselves." Lolo Sebyo follows my gaze. He heaves a heavy sigh. "I tried to heal Toyang, but she didn't want me to dabble with the complexities of magic that involve matters of life and death. If the person I wanted to heal rejected my magic, it would not work. Consent is what separates healing magic from self-serving magic. There are gray areas, but taking someone's right to choose usually ends up with terrible consequences."

"I see." An idea then pops into my head. "Lolo, if magic can make someone happy, can it make someone kind too? Like, stop them from being mean?"

"Is someone being mean to you in school?" Lolo Sebyo asks, frowning.

"No." I feel guilty for lying, but I don't want to get my grandfather involved. Who knows what Claudine would do? She already threatened to endanger Mom's job. Besides, it's not 100 percent a lie. Claudine isn't my classmate at school. She's just part of my Bible study group. "I'm just curious."

Well, that's also true.

Lolo Sebyo still looks a bit suspicious, but I can see the worry leaving his face. "Yes, magic can bring out kindness, but it will only work properly on people who are already kind deep down and simply needed the push."

"That doesn't make any sense. Why would anyone who's already kind need a push to be kind?"

"Perhaps they are so used to being unkind that being kind is hard." Lolo Sebyo peers at me and tilts his head. "However, as an arbularyo, it is important to know when it's unnecessary to use magic. We shouldn't rely on magic all the time. For example, the kindness potion. You need to ask your client if they have first tried being kind to the other person. Kindness usually begets kindness. It's only when all other options fail that we might consider using magic to coax their buried kindness out."

I hide my disappointment. "But what if the other person just isn't kind?"

"Then the magic won't work properly, if at all." Lolo Sebyo puts a filled potion bottle in a tiny bag. "In those cases, we—"

"PAPA! WHERE ARE YOU? I'M DYING HERE!"

I giggle as I watch Lolo Sebyo struggling not to roll his eyes.

"Rainier knows exactly where I am," he says, shaking his head. "Your father is so melodramatic. Dinner rush won't kill him."

Before his stroke, Lolo Sebyo was also a tricycle driver aside from being an arbularyo. Lola Toyang ran the family's eatery, the Bagayan Food Haus. It sells home-cooked meals to the fisherfolk and their families. Then Lola Toyang passed away, and now it's my dad who manages the eatery with Lolo Sebyo helping him take orders during rush hours.

To be fair, I don't think Lolo has any idea what to do in the canteen. He's like Mom—they're both terrible cooks.

"Clean the palayok before you leave, my Bee. And be quick! It seems we need all hands on deck at the canteen," says Lolo Sebyo. He nods in Kidlat's direction as he opens the door. "Watch over my granddaughter, you brave good boy."

As I scrub the palayok, I think about Claudine and this kindness potion Lolo Sebyo mentioned. Could it be that she is just used to being unkind and simply needs a little prodding? It's a bit of a stretch, but it's worth a try.

CHAPTER FOUR

Nanay Dadang's Sari-Sari Store

One thing I like about Isla Pag-Ibig is being able to walk home with Kidlat during the week. I'll take a tricycle from school to Nanay Dadang's, where he patiently waits for me. We'll walk the remaining kilometer going home together. If I have extra allowance money, like today, we munch on ice candies during our journey.

I could never do something like this when we still lived in Manila. The house we rented there was in a not-so-pleasant neighborhood. For my safety, Mom accompanied me on the way to school and going home. Instead of tall coconut trees lining a dirt road, we'd have to go past street vendors hawking pirated wares and cheap knockoffs. There, we heard police sirens from antidrug operations. But here, there's only the soft trickling of the roadside creek and the occasional roar of a tricycle's motorcycle engine.

"Hey, good boy!" I hurry to meet my dog after school on Monday. As usual, he's sitting patiently at the store. On either side of him are two sleeping Muscovy ducks. The ducks are so used to seeing people come up to the general store that they barely budge when I come bounding down.

"Jolina Beatrice!" A woman's high-pitched voice chirps from behind the counter—Nanay Dadang's. She emerges from a cluster of hanging potato chip bags and sampler-sized shampoos. "You're late. Your dog has been waiting for you for thirty minutes. Wouldn't move even when I told it to go home."

"Hi, Nanay Dadang. Thanks for letting him stay." I greet the old lady, bringing out a couple of ten-peso coins. This is another thing I love about moving to a rural town. Everyone knows everyone else. I haven't been here long, and yet Nanay Dadang already treats Kidlat and me like family. "Can I have some ice candies please? Chocolate for me, sugar-free papaya for the pup."

"Ay! Your grandfather will have my head if he finds out I've been selling you ice candies." Nanay Dadang sells me the ice candies anyway. "Here, have another chocolate. I know you love them. And some mineral water. You have a long walk going home. You live in a canteen and yet you are still so thin!"

I'm used to Nanay Dadang's unflattering comments. I know better than to answer back in a disrespectful way.

"Thank you." I tear the plastic off the tip of the home-made ice candy and take a bite. Yum. So chocolatey! "It's genetic po. I got my thinness from Mom."

"Sus!" Nanay Dadang waves her hand. "*Science-schmience*. In my day, we just ate a lot. Worked a lot too."

"Can I also buy a mobile load?" I give her another wad of bills. "Just fifty pesos po."

Nanay Dadang switches to complaining about technology. But just like with the ice candies, she still sells me a prepaid load. "Say hello to your grandfather for me! You children nowadays do nothing but play those things on your phone—"

"Hi, Nanay Dadang!" an all-too-familiar voice chirps behind me.

Ugh. I groan inwardly as I unwrap Kidlat's papaya ice candy and hand it to him.

Claudine. She wasn't at Bible study yesterday (which I was happy about). But now here she is again, like there's just no way to escape her.

"Oh, hello, dear," Nanay Dadang greets back. She pokes her head out of the sari-sari store's small window. "That looks dangerous. What do you call that thing? Should you even be riding that?"

I stifle a giggle, stuffing my mouth with chocolate ice candy so I don't need to say anything. Nanay Dadang looks like Lola Sebyo's chicken with its head poking out of its cage.

"It's an electric scooter. An e-scooter," Claudine answers with a grin. Her eyes meet mine briefly, and I can see them twinkle. She must be thinking the same thing of Nanay Dadang. "It's perfectly safe. You know how Mommy is—she'd never let me anywhere near anything dangerous. May I have a bottle of water and a pack of yema balls, please?"

I might be wrong about her. Maybe Claudine really is kind, deep inside. And it looks like she's in a good mood today.

"Here you go, anak," Nanay Dadang says, referring to Claudine as her child. "Do you want anything else?"

"I'm okay." Claudine parks her electric scooter by the store's wooden benches. I've always wanted one of those but they're too expensive. Claudine downs the mineral water in one gulp. She removes the colored wrapper from the yema and pops into her mouth the sweet, custard-like candy encased in a crunchy, caramel shell.

"Do you know Jolina?" Nanay Dadang's face lights up. "She's Sunshine Bagayan's daughter."

"Opo." Claudine nods as she pays for her bottled water. She eats another yema ball. "Sunshine is a receptionist trainee at my mommy's resort."

I purse my lips. Never mind. Maybe she's not so nice, after all.

I'm not sure if it's the fact that Claudine calls my mother

by her first name. Or the fact that she just implied *again* that my family is beneath her. Or both. Either way, Claudine is getting on my nerves once more—even after I promised myself I wouldn't let her. Being kind to a person like this is next to impossible.

It's time for me to leave before I say anything mean.

"Have to go. Bye, Nanay Dadang!" I jog after my dog, who's already halfway down the dirt road. He only slows down when Nanay Dadang and Claudine can't possibly see us anymore.

"Hey, wait up!"

Kidlat and I turn around and find Claudine riding her e-scooter toward us. She slams the breaks, showering my shoes with tiny pebbles.

"Hi—"

"Why do you have to be so rude to Nanay Dadang?" Claudine keeps her left hand on the scooter while placing the other one on her hip.

"Rude? Me?" Seriously? *She* thinks *I* was the rude one? "*You* were rude about my mom."

"I wasn't," insists Claudine. Her eyes narrow. "Nanay Dadang just asked me if I knew you're her daughter. She didn't know Sunshine works at Mommy's resort."

I'm trying not to let my temper get the best of me, but Claudine is making it really, really hard. "Please stop calling my mother by her first name. She's older than you. In

Manila, we don't call adults by their first names. I would think you should know better."

"Argh!" Claudine pulls on her hair, letting her scooter fall to the ground. "Manila, Manila, Manila. I am so tired of hearing you say you came from Manila. Just stop it already!"

Claudine's outburst startles Kidlat. He lets out a low growl as he presses against my leg protectively.

"Shh." I hush my dog, taking deep breaths to calm my racing heart. I totally get Kidlat's anger—I have to leave now before I say anything I'll regret later on. Mom's job depends on it.

I spy a dirt path near the creek—a trail that leads straight to our village, Barangay San Pedro. A trail where Claudine can't follow us with her expensive scooter. "We're going home."

"For your information, I called your mother Tita Sunshine when we first met," Claudine calls behind my back. Maybe it's wishful thinking, but I think I hear a hint of desperation in her voice. "She's the one who insisted I call her Sunshine. Ask her if you don't believe me."

Yeah, right. Mom is the one who taught me about using honorifics to show respect for our elders. Whether it's someone really old like Lolo Sebyo, or someone just a few years older than me—they deserve to be treated and referred to with respect.

This girl doesn't have a shred of kindness. She keeps making excuses to pick a fight. She wants me to say something mean so she can go running to her mother and get my mom fired.

I'm never, *ever* going to let that happen.

CHAPTER FIVE

Daughter of Rain and Sunshine

The moon's almost out when Kidlat and I arrive home. My dog heads straight for the backyard gate to herd Lolo's chickens. Kidlat doesn't like seeing the chickens running about. Based on the sounds of loud flapping and angry clucks from the yard, I'm pretty sure the chickens don't like him either.

Our home is like most of the houses in the area—old, Spanish-era houses reinforced with concrete to withstand weathering from the sun and the sea. The only difference is that our eatery takes up the entire front of our house and we have a potion lab at the back.

I pass by the empty tables on the front patio and enter the eatery. Bagayan Food Haus is usually empty at this time. Dinner fare has replaced the afternoon snack options on the counter, ready for the early evening crowd arriving around six.

Lolo Sebyo is behind the cash register. But he's not alone.

A woman who looks a bit older than my mother is talking to him. She's dressed simply in a plain blouse and a pleated skirt.

"Come on, Tatay Sebyo," the woman pleads with my grandfather. "I'll even double the amount. Two thousand pesos."

Lolo Sebyo shakes his head. "I'm sorry, Nadia. I cannot make one for you."

Oh. I guess this woman needs Lolo's arbularyo services. Out of respect, I hang back and take a seat near the end of the counter. Bagayan Food Haus is a small eatery, so I can hear everything they say without even trying.

"Three thousand," the woman says. "Please."

"No, my child." Lolo's voice is firm. "My conscience cannot handle seeing you live with the consequences of using a love potion to forcibly take someone's property. Hire a lawyer. From what you told me, you have legal rights to it."

The woman sighs loudly. "But it would take too long!"

"Indeed, but it is the right and lawful way."

"Can't you just—just one drop of gayuma," says the woman. She reaches over the counter to take my grandpa's hand. "Please, Tatay Sebyo."

"I am sorry." Lolo Sebyo pats her hand in return. "I cannot help you."

The woman looks like she's about to try again but thinks

better of it. She bids Lolo Sebyo goodbye, and he gives her his blessing. My grandfather says he will pray for her. Not only for her to settle her problems, but for her to be able to find peace as well.

As soon as she's out of earshot, I approach the cash register. "Why didn't you want to make a love potion for her, Lolo?"

"The gayuma is a dangerous potion, my Bee." Lolo Sebyo's lips turn to a grim line. "It is called a 'love potion,' but is love still love when forced upon someone else? And using 'love' to get what you want is wrong. Very wrong."

"But—"

"Come now, Bee. Go to your father," Lolo Sebyo says, his voice as firm as the tone he used on the woman. "I believe he is cooking ube halaya and might need your help."

I do as I'm told. I know better than to bother Lolo when he's upset. Especially when he's upset because he had to turn down helping someone. As an arbularyo-in-training, this is what I'm in for. I hope I'll be ready for it.

"In here, sweetheart," Dad calls from the kitchen, where he's peeling boiled ube roots. "There's adobo and caldereta at the eatery."

I dump my backpack on the sofa.

"Mano po," I say, asking for his hand. Dad responds by ruffling my hair with his clean hand. "Thanks, Dad."

The door connecting our house to the eatery opens. Mom emerges, still clad in her work uniform—blue denim shorts and a collared, bright yellow polo shirt. She greets Dad and me with quick kisses, then heads for the sofa to remove her shoes and untie her ponytail.

Like me, my mother is small and thin. Well, I'm more on the scrawny side. But we have the same build, so hopefully I'll fill out a bit when I grow up. Mom has a high-bridged nose and big eyes and lighter-than-usual brown skin. Most people say her mouth is her best feature, and I agree with them. Her lips are red and pouty and always ready to curve into a smile.

My mother deserves the name Sunshine. She can brighten up any dreary room just by being there.

"Where's Kidlat? That dog didn't greet me hello yet." Mom retrieves a squeak-less dog toy from under the bamboo frame of the sofa and places it on the table. The stuffed turtle toy didn't use to be squeak-less. It squeaked a lot, and loudly too. Kidlat made it squeak so much that Mom gave the toy surgery to remove the thing that made the squeaking sound. It's been squeak-less since then, but Kidlat still adores it.

"He's outside chasing chickens."

"Jolina! Lolo Sebyo loves those birds—"

"I know, Mom." I hold up my hands in surrender, laughing. "I'm kidding."

Well, I'm only half kidding. Kidlat *was* chasing the chickens, but by this time, he is sleeping on the picnic table under the mango tree. It's his favorite afternoon siesta place.

Mom rolls her eyes but grins at me. "Silly girl. You're just like your dad—"

"Hey!" Dad protests as he finishes peeling the last of the boiled ube roots. He then disappears behind the counter. When he emerges, he's carrying a huge, empty vat.

"Need help?" Mom asks my father as she slips her feet into her flip-flops.

"I got this, hon," says Dad. "Almost done."

As fate would have it, Dad's name is Rainier, or Rain for short. Maybe it's just a coincidence, but it's cool to think that I'm the daughter of Rain and Sunshine.

I ask for Mom's hand and she chucks my chin in response. "How was school?"

School was usual as far as school in Isla Pag-Ibig goes. As always, no one bothered talking to me. Well, a class-mate or two said "excuse me" or asked me to pass a paper. Other than that, I spent recess alone. I guess no one really wants to befriend the dayo.

But my parents don't need to know that. "It was okay."

Mom raises her eyebrows. "Only okay?"

Ugh. Why do parents have this superpower of knowing that things aren't okay even when we kids say they are?

"Well, I aced another test." I have to give her something, or she'll never stop asking. "I didn't even study for it!"

"You truly are my daughter." Dad grins. "Too smart for school."

Mom shakes a finger at me. "Don't get used to it. It'll get more challenging, I promise."

I pour myself an orange juice from the fridge. From the corner of my eye, I can see Mom massaging her legs while Dad smashes ube roots in the vat with butter and condensed milk.

We didn't use to be like this, you know. It's hard to believe that only a few months have passed since Lola Toyang went to Heaven. And Dad was still the head chef of the hotel where Mom worked as a manager.

We had to sell a lot of our stuff to help pay for Lola Toyang's cancer treatment. Then we moved here. Now Lola Toyang is gone, Dad is only a cook at his family's eatery, and Mom is just a receptionist-on-probation at a mean girl's family resort.

Claudine is a mean girl through and through. She knows she gets to me. Every time she sees I'm affected by the awful things she says, Claudine just provokes me even more.

I don't need her meanness in my life. My family has been through so much already. I don't want to add to Mom and Dad's burden by making them worry about me having a rough time adjusting to life here.

Starting today, I will not let Claudine Dimasalang bother me. I'm going to ignore her, like she doesn't exist. Maybe then she'll get tired and finally leave me alone.

CHAPTER SIX

The Best Party of the Year

One of the things I really miss about Manila is having my own desk in school. My parents were able to send me to a private Catholic school with Lolo Sebyo and Lola Toyang's help. But being on an island province like Isla Pag-Ibig—it's different. There aren't any private schools. Just public schools where I have to share my desk with two other kids who don't seem to want anything to do with me.

Sunday school's setup is more similar to that of my school in Manila. There aren't many of us who attend it since some kids prefer to have mass instead of Bible study. I get to have my own desk in the corner of the room and avoid Claudine.

Well . . . I try to, at least.

"Hi." A tall, dark boy comes up to my desk. I don't

really know him, but we go to the same public school. I heard his friends call him Marvin. The other kids seem to like him enough, but he's never said a word to me. Until now, that is.

"Hi," I say back. I try to think of what to say next. I promised myself I'd make an effort to be friendlier, but I really have no idea what else to say.

Marvin gestures to the desk on my left. "Is this seat taken?"

"No."

"Can I sit here?"

"Okay."

"Thanks." Marvin looks like he's about to say something more, but he just closes his mouth. He turns to the short-haired Chinese Filipino girl wearing glasses sitting on his other side. I can't remember her name. Angela or Angelica or something.

Ugh. I'll try again later. I'm sure we'll have more to talk about once the catechist hands out the activity sheets for the day.

At exactly three o'clock, Claudine saunters in. She takes a handful of yema balls from the candy bowl on our catechist's table, claiming the desk right in front of it. She turns to face us and waves a bunch of small white envelopes. "Guess who's having the best party of the year soon."

As Claudine distributes the envelopes, everyone, including Marvin and Angela/Angelica, talks excitedly among themselves. Everyone but me.

I chew on my fingernails as Claudine draws near. I know I said I don't care about her anymore, but it would be so embarrassing if everyone got an invite and I didn't. And I love parties. I always got invited to parties back in Manila.

"What do people do at parties here anyway?" I ask Marvin and Angela/Angelica. "Do you guys sing videoke all day?"

The two kids laugh. *Progress!*

"Not all day, no," Marvin says with a grin. "We also—"

"Do stuff that you'll only hear about but will not see," Claudine finishes for him. She hands Marvin and Angela/Angelica an envelope each but keeps the last one under her arm. "You're not invited."

I feel like I've been punched in the gut. Considering our recent fight at Nanay Dadang's, I shouldn't be surprised that she's not inviting me. But it still hurts not to be included. Like, it really hurts.

But I don't care. I don't care. *I don't care.*

I've told myself I won't care about what she thinks, says, or does. I don't care if she's embarrassing me in front of everyone.

Claudine Dimasalang doesn't exist to me.

"Um, Claudine . . ." Angela/Angelica clears her throat. "Maybe you can make room for one more—"

"No." Claudine glares at me as she waves the last envelope. "This is for Mr. Bradbury. He may have started as a dayo here, but he sure doesn't act like we're beneath him. Unlike this *Manilenya* here who thinks she's better than everyone just because she lived in the capital. You want to know what's going to happen at my party?"

"I don't," I croak, a lump in my throat forming. I can feel everyone's eyes on me. "I don't care."

"I'm going to tell you anyway." Claudine's lips curve into a sneer. "My guests are going to stuff themselves silly with this *amazing* international buffet. Mommy hired a magician and a petting zoo—I heard they're bringing a monkey and a cockatoo and a giant snake. We'll have free-flowing ice cream and cotton candy and french fries and fish balls. Everyone is invited *but you*."

I bite my lower lip, blinking hard to stop myself from crying. I love cotton candy and fish balls. And the petting zoo sounds exciting—I've never seen a monkey, a cockatoo, or a giant snake up close. It sounds like the kind of party I'd love to attend, but I'm not invited.

Claudine Dimasalang is such an expert at making me feel less than I really am. Maybe in some alternate universe, I'm rich and she's poor. But even then, I'm 100 percent sure she'd still manage to make me feel like a lesser human being.

Through my wet eyes, I see the other kids looking at me. But not one of them says anything to Claudine.

They're scared of her.

Well, I'm not scared of her. I'm Jolina Beatrice Bagayan,

arbularyo apprentice. I'm not afraid of this silly, mean girl. "What did I ever do to you?"

Claudine's eyes narrow. "It's so obvious—"

Dong! Dong! Dong!

Saved by the church bell. Everyone runs back to their seats, even Claudine. No one wants to be caught bullying me when Mr. Terrence Bradbury, our volunteer catechist, arrives.

A tear runs down my cheek. I brush it away before anyone sees.

Whatever is obvious to Claudine, I'll never know. And I really, honest-to-goodness don't care. Because as of this moment, I'm decided.

Claudine is going to get what she deserves. Whether she likes it or not.

Seven Steps to Gayuma Making

It isn't easy finding a gayuma spell in Lolo Sebyo's library. Considering how he feels about using the love potion, I'm not surprised. It's hidden on the lowest shelf with the dirtiest, most neglected ancient books. And the only one I find is in a thin red book that contains a single gayuma recipe and pages upon pages of ridiculous love advice from one of our old arbularyo ancestors in the early 1900s.

Gayuma: Love Potion
A Recipe by Antonio Bagayan IV

Greetings, dear arbularyo! So, you want to make a love potion. Perhaps it is for a lovestruck client, or a poor soul whose heart you would like to help heal—I shall not judge you. Your reasons are your business. Truth be told, it is not of any concern to me.

However, I shall make it my concern to ask you if you are aware of what you are about to do.

It will take anywhere from a moment to a day for the gayuma to take effect. Your power as an arbularyo will dictate how long it takes.

It is very difficult to discern love from gayuma and real, un-magicked love. Its effects on the target have been characterized as constantly thinking about the client and the unquestioning deference of the target to the client. Rest assured, any other person who unwittingly takes the gayuma will be unaffected. The magic only applies to your target.

Do not forget to say protective prayers on yourself as the brewer and ask for the Lord's blessing when you are through. Just like any brew, be sure to offer Him everything you do. Then you may proceed.

Herewith are the ingredients of the brew:

A pink candle

A bundle of herbs for emotion alteration

Two drops of Positive Thinking

Half a drop of Persuasive Speech

A thornless red rose

A teaspoon of raw sugar

A dash of sea salt

A photograph of the intended target

A delivery vessel

The delivery vessel you use must be an edible food that the target willingly ingests. If the target does not eat it, your gayuma serves no purpose.

Heed my warning, my fellow arbularyo. Love is a powerful force, as is magic. Two powerful forces combined in a potion can result in even greater consequences. It is unlike any potion you will ever brew; its magic different from what you are used to.

Be certain to remind your client that magic is a covenant. What magic gives, magic will eventually take.

The book is obviously warning about Balik. Every arbularyo knows this. Even I already know this. It's the most basic rule of magic—you reap what you sow. "Balik" directly translates as "return." Do good, get good returns. Do bad, get bad returns.

But Lolo Sebyo always says an arbularyo is protected by God from dark forces if they intend to help, not hurt. And how could I be doing bad by helping Claudine be a better person?

So I want justice too. Isn't justice good? What Claudine did to me in Sunday school was wrong. Lolo Sebyo may not approve, but I believe this is the only way.

Besides, if my Bagayan ancestors have brewed gayuma, the Balik couldn't be that bad, right? Our entire clan would have been wiped out of existence with all the bad karma coming from every Bagayan who makes a gayuma.

It's for the greater good. I'm not the only one who would benefit from a kinder, more loving Claudine. Everyone in Bible study group who's terrified of her will too. And I'm going to make sure I take the proper precautions. My brewing skills might be at a less-than-proficient level, but the book does say gayuma magic is very different. Maybe that also means this magic won't reject me as much as the magic I've been trying to learn. For once, I might make a potion that actually works.

Because I need it to work.

It has to.

* * *

The ingredients of the gayuma are surprisingly easy to acquire. Granted, I'm an arbularyo's apprentice and I know where to get magical herbs easily. I have seen bottles of Positive Thinking and Persuasive Speech potions in Lolo's cabinet. I only need a few drops, so I'm sure he won't notice if I take some.

I don't want to blow my allowance on buying gayuma stuff, so I make do with what I have. Like the pink candle, for example. It just says that the candle needs to be colored pink. Lolo Sebyo's potion book doesn't mention anything specific except for that.

So I melt a white candle and a pink crayon, combining them together to make a pink candle. Simple.

Well, except for the unexpected challenge that is Kidlat.

"Kidlat, no!" I jump as my dog pushes my thighs with his front paws. "I'll play with you later. I might burn myself if you don't behave."

The dog's ears flatten on his head, his tail lowered. He lets out a long, loud whine. But he stops bothering me. Before long, I have a thick, foot-long pink candle. I hide it in my dresser until I'm ready to brew.

Getting Claudine's photo is trickier though.

It's been a week since Claudine embarrassed me in front of everyone, and in that time, I've managed to ignore her. Every now and then, she'll be at Nanay Dadang's store buying random things like chips and batteries, but I pretend not to see her. Sometimes I'll catch her looking at me. I don't know why and I really don't care, but it does pose a problem in getting her photo without her noticing.

I get my chance after Sunday school, when we're both waiting for our moms to pick us up.

I act like I'm taking a photo of the church and landscape behind it. But Claudine is watching me.

"If you keep taking my picture, I'm going to have to charge you a talent fee," Claudine quips. She pouts and sticks her hips in an exaggerated pose.

I hide my laugh in a snort. Claudine is actually funny when she's not being a brat.

Then I remember what she did to me last Sunday.

"What do you know about talent fees? There aren't any modeling agencies here," I snap back. I feel guilty instantly. Even for me, that's really mean.

Claudine's face turns bright red. "My cousin is a model. She lives in Makati City. You're not the only one who's been to Manila, dayo."

I open my mouth to apologize but close it immediately. I haven't forgotten how she embarrassed me. She made me look like an unwanted piece of dry buko pie in front of everyone, with her non-invite.

"It's not illegal to take photos of the church," I say, while taking *another* photo of the church. I make sure Claudine's face is sharp and clear in the foreground.

Claudine flips her hair. She's sporting pink-and-green highlights today. "For you, everything should be illegal."

Whatever. I take another photo just for good measure. Easy-peasy.

The hardest part of making gayuma is actually brewing the gayuma itself. Once I have all the ingredients that can't be found in Lolo's lab, I need to be able to brew the love potion without my grandfather knowing. But like with getting Claudine's photo, I just need to wait for the perfect moment.

I'm outside Lolo Sebyo's lab with Kidlat in tow when my grandfather sees us.

Ugh. Kidlat's whining is so loud, I'm surprised the whole neighborhood doesn't see us. My dog has been acting weird every time I do anything related to this gayuma project.

"What are you up to, curious Bee?" he asks as he unlocks the lab.

"Nothing much." I feel terrible lying to my grandfather, but it's the only way I can make this gayuma plan work. "I'm done with my homework. Can I borrow some books on protective potions? I think I can do the spell version easily. But I want to read ahead on potions so I don't blow up your house when we have our lesson this Saturday."

It's not totally a lie. I do want to read up on protective potions for our next lesson. Just not today.

"So studious, just like your father. Rainier would have been a great arbularyo had he not preferred the cooking over magic." Lolo Sebyo waves me in. "Keep it up, my Bee. You're going to be a great arbularyo one day. Perhaps even the best of our clan. You have your key?"

I nod.

"Good. Don't forget to lock up. I need to buy some vegetables for your father."

Lolo Sebyo's so genuinely trusting of me that I feel another stab of guilt. Then I remember how mean Claudine was. Not just to me, but to everyone around her. I'm doing the right thing.

Time to brew this gayuma.

CHAPTER EIGHT

The Arbularyo's Apprentice

Herbs? Check.

Pink candle? Rose? Salt and sugar? Check.

Target's image? I place the printed photo of Claudine on the table. Check.

Prayer? I load the notes application on my phone and pull up the prayer I scoured from Lolo Sebyo's library. Check.

Positive Thinking and Persuasive Speech potions? All stored in little bottles on Lolo Sebyo's shelf, waiting for me to take. Check.

An empty potion lab? Lolo Sebyo left the house to run some errands in town, while Dad is busy preparing the canteen's lunch menu. Mom is still working at Claudine's family resort.

Check, check, check.

I'm so ready.

Based on my research, the "delivery vessel" is the medium I'll use to give Claudine the gayuma. So for this, I'm making yema balls. It's a dessert traditionally based on egg yolks, milk, and sugar. I find the custard candy too sweet for my taste, especially when it has a hard caramel shell instead of the simple white sugar coating of my family's recipe. But Claudine obviously loves it. Whenever I see Claudine at Nanay Dadang's, she's eating those candy balls one after the other.

As I open cans of condensed milk, I remember how Mom brought these candies for Claudine a few months back. It's as if Mom needs to give that family "offerings" while she is at their mercy. Whether or not Mom gets promoted to a regular position depends on their whims. Her expertise in hospitality management means nothing if she doesn't suck up to the Dimasalangs—Claudine included.

I may have magic, but Claudine's family has money, the kind of power I need for my family's life to be better. I feel so powerful and so powerless at the same time.

It's so unfair.

Anyway, the cooking part is also the step in gayuma making that I find the easiest and the most fun. It's like science. Not *science* science like physics and biology and stuff but science nonetheless.

You see, food reacts in different ways. Bad combinations result in gross food. A wrong temperature can burn a stew. Cause and effect—it's all science.

Interesting how very similar science and magic are.

Kidlat's barking interrupts my thoughts. He growls at the magic palayok in front of me.

"You don't understand," I tell my dog. "This isn't just about me."

Kidlat is a very smart dog. He's just looking out for me. But I wish he'd be more supportive. And less judgy. I feel like every time I'm doing something gayuma related, Kidlat is judging me.

I probably shouldn't be cooking without the adults around, but this is the only time I can make the love potion without them asking questions. I feel bad about it, but like I keep reminding myself—*this isn't just for me, but for everyone else.*

I stir the condensed milk, egg yolks, and calamansi juice slowly over low heat with a wooden ladle. Traditionally, this candy is made with milk and sugar instead of condensed milk, but I find condensed milk richer in texture. The tangy juice of Philippine lime gives the candy a hint of zest. This recipe is what Lola Toyang taught me, and it's also what Dad uses for the candies we sell at the canteen. It's the same recipe that makes the best yema in the entire province of Isla Pag-Ibig.

The mixture thickens as it cooks. Like, really thickens. I add the gayuma ingredients except for the half drop of Persuasive Speech. The yema-gayuma mixture thickens even more, making it harder to stir.

But I like the grunt work. It helps me channel my anger at the mean things Claudine said.

Your mother works for my family.

You're so rude.

You'll always be a dayo.

You're not invited.

With each phrase, I turn the ladle, channeling my anger in cooking.

Then, finally, I add the half drop of Persuasive Speech. The potion hisses, and Kidlat whines once more.

"Shh, Kidlat," I shush him. "We're almost done."

I whisper my prayer and end it the way Lolo Sebyo concludes his chants. "Ang lahat ng ito ay alay namin sa inyo, Panginoon."

The thick yema-gayuma mixture bubbles and emits black smoke.

"Oh no!" I hope I don't make anything explode. Brewing isn't my strongest talent, but I know I've followed the gayuma recipe to the letter. I must have overcooked the yema! It doesn't smell like it's burning though—more like rotten eggs and spoiled milk.

Gross.

As I turn off the stove, the smoke suddenly turns pink. The icky smell is gone, and it's replaced by the pleasant scent of freshly picked roses.

"Perfect!"

I transfer the yema custard mixture to a butter-lined plate

to cool. I glance at the clock and see that I still have three hours before we leave for church this afternoon. Three hours to scoop and roll the custard candies, dredge them in granulated white sugar, and wrap them individually for Claudine.

Let's face it, I'm not really good at this. But the gayuma might just work. And if it does, I'm going to have a new "friend" who "loves" me. It's obviously not real—just a temporary fix like Lolo says. But this year has been so difficult for me and my family that it's nice to be able to look forward to something for once.

CHAPTER NINE

Bagayan's Best
Yema Balls

At exactly three o'clock, Claudine arrives at Bible study.

"Well, well, well. Look who's early today!" Claudine drawls. She really is a creature of habit.

I nibble my fingers nervously as Claudine takes a bunch of yema candies from the bowl on the catechist's desk. I'm hoping she won't notice that the wrappers of the gayuma-ed version are different from the rest of the candies.

It's risky, putting the gayuma out in the open like that. But I can't think of any other way Claudine can get these candies. It's not like I can break into Nanay Dadang's sari-sari store and replace her yema supply with mine.

Thankfully, the gayuma book said that it doesn't matter if everyone eats the delivery vessel. Only Claudine will experience the potion's effects.

"Are you going to my party?" Claudine stops in front of the desk of one of the Sunday-school boys. I'm not good with remembering people's names, but it's easy to remember Bobby's because he's always nice to me. Bobby is a chubby boy with a kind smile. He doesn't talk much, so I try not to bother him. Claudine doesn't believe in letting others be, apparently.

"Yes," croaks Bobby. If I'm not mistaken, he's actually scared of saying no. "I am."

"You're going to have so much fun at my party," Claudine gushes. "I can't even with the yummy food Mommy ordered!"

Bobby leans back into his chair like he doesn't want Claudine too near. Still, he gives the taller girl a smile. "I can't wait."

Claudine goes on and on about her party to anyone who'll listen. Some, like the twins Judy and Ann, seem genuinely interested. But the others are like Bobby—just scared to say anything that'll anger Claudine.

The party does sound fun, like it's really going to be the best party of the year, as Claudine brags. But I'm not invited—yet.

If all goes well, I might find myself having fish balls at that party after all.

"Don't let it get to you." Angela/Angelica slides into the desk beside me.

"Huh?"

"Claudine." Marvin takes the table next to Angela/ Angelica. He throws a wary glance in Claudine's direction. "Angelou's right. You should just avoid her when she gets like that."

Oh. *Angelou* is Angela/Angelica's name.

"Anyway, we've been around Claudine long enough to know that ayaw niya ng pagbabago," Angelou continues. "She doesn't like change. You being here is a huge change."

Yep. Like I said, Claudine is a creature of habit. Still—

"Oh, hello there! Good afternoon, kiddos. How are you today?" Mr. Bradbury enters the room. He's a tall, muscular Black man with broad shoulders, and he sports a military-style haircut. He has a goatee that I usually see on musicians. Mr. Bradbury gives Claudine a smile. "You're keeping busy, I see."

"Thanks, Mr. Bradbury. This is so delish. More than usual, actually." Claudine crumples a pale blue wrapper. My pulse quickens. She's eating the yema balls I made. "Mmm . . . This is really good."

Mr. Bradbury takes a candy and pops it into his mouth. I hope to Papa Jesus the gayuma book is right and gayuma only affects the target. "You're right. It is heavenly. It's like the candies Nanay Toyang made. This is a Bagayan Food Haus yema ball!"

I hide my gasp with a fake cough. I'm doomed—

"I must have had some left from the pack I bought yesterday." Mr. Bradbury shrugs. The panic in my face clears, and I heave a huge sigh of relief. The catechist smiles at me. "Your family's yema balls really are the best."

"Thanks, Mr. Bradbury," I manage to croak with a smile. Thank goodness he doesn't know how cold my hands are.

They have no idea I made the yema balls.

I'm a nervous wreck, but hearing them compliment my cooking gives me an odd feeling of pride.

Mr. Bradbury grins back at Claudine. He brings out a poster and flattens it on the board with one hand. From what I've heard, he lost half his left arm during a tour in Afghanistan. He was a soldier for the US Army until he found his calling to be a soldier of the Lord. His background reminds me of the story of Saint Ignatius of Loyola—Dad and Lolo Sebyo's favorite saint. "Okay! Today we will discuss Genesis 3, the Fall of Man. Open your Bibles and let us discuss why there is evil in the world and why we need Jesus to save us. Claudine, can you hand me the tape—"

But Marvin is faster than Claudine. He's by Mr. Bradbury's side before he can even finish his sentence.

I roll my eyes. Talk about obvious.

I glance at Claudine. She's rolling her eyes too.

We share a knowing smirk. It's almost as if we're actually friends even after the whole non-invite incident.

Then Claudine scowls. She takes the Bible from her bag, which was hanging on her backrest.

Never mind.

Sighing, I turn my Bible to the correct page.

The gayuma book said it can take up to a full day before the magic takes effect. I'm far from being a powerful arbularyo, so for now, all I can do is wait.

CHAPTER TEN

BFFAE: Best Friends Forever And Ever

It's now Tuesday, and I still haven't heard anything from Claudine. The gayuma should have taken effect by now.

The book said that the maximum time for the gayuma to start taking effect is an entire day, depending on my skills as an arbularyo. But it also said gayuma magic is different. I can't be such a horrible arbularyo that even gayuma magic rejects me, can I?

Since yesterday, Kidlat and I have been hanging out longer at Nanay Dadang's sari-sari store, waiting for Claudine. But she's nowhere to be found.

"Sa dalas mong tumambay dito, malapit na kitang igawa ng sarili mong bench," Nanay Dadang quips, telling me that I hang out so much there, soon she'll need to make me my own bench. "A young lady like yourself should spend more time with kids your age. You might end up an old spinster like my sister if you keep that up!"

Her sister, Nanay Concha, rolls her eyes. "Eh ano naman kung maging matandang dalaga sya? So what if she becomes an old spinster? You should be grateful I didn't marry, or you'd have been left alone when your husband died!"

"Sus!" Nanay Dadang gives her a dismissive wave. "You would have brought your entire family to live with me. Your conscience would not be able to handle leaving your ate alone."

"That's what you think." Nanay Concha winks as she hands me some ice candies.

"*Sus!*" Nanay Dadang rolls her eyes once more before she heads to the back of the store. It's obvious that they're just having fun.

Nanay Dadang can be rude sometimes (I honestly like her sister better and wish she were at the store more often), but I enjoy watching and listening to them squabble. It must be nice to have a sister.

"Don't mind her. It is perfectly fine to be alone. Just do what makes you happy."

"Thank you po, but I'm not alone," I tell her, smiling. I lean down to stroke Kidlat's soft fur.

"That is true." Nanay Concha smiles back. She cocks her head to the side. "Still . . . are you waiting for somebody? You have that same look this fella gets when you're not here yet."

"Um . . . I'm not—" I bite my lower lip. Old people like to gossip in this town. I don't want the entire island to know I'm looking for Claudine. I'm pretty certain I've been careful and said all the protective prayers, but I have to be sure nothing bad happened to her. After all, I did give her gayuma. "Have you seen Claudine?"

"The Dimasalang girl?"

I nod. Thank goodness Nanay Concha doesn't ask too many questions.

To my disappointment, she shakes her head. "Not lately."

"How about Nanay Dadang?" I ask as casually as possible, even when my heart is beating so fast, I can barely breathe.

"No. I believe the last time the girl was here was Sunday morning."

Sunday morning. My stomach turns. That was before I gave Claudine the gayuma. No one has seen her since she's had it.

I hope she'll eventually turn up. But Friday comes and goes—still no Claudine.

By Saturday morning, I'm a total mess. I make so many mistakes in my magic lesson with Lolo Sebyo that he ends our session early.

"Your mind is obviously elsewhere," he says. "Why don't you head out early? I still have to brew a potion for Tonio's son. Poor child must have run afoul with an angry engkanto."

I tell Lolo making an anti-angry-engkanto potion sounds fun, but Lolo refuses to let me stay.

I try to help Dad in the eatery, but even there I'm too distracted. I almost add an entire pan of mashed boiled liver into a vat of macaroni salad. I could have seriously destroyed a perfectly good batch of macaroni salad. It's a sin to ruin macaroni salad that way, not to mention really gross.

By Sunday afternoon, I'm a wreck. I'm convinced something did happen to Claudine. I didn't want to bring Mom into this and give her unnecessary worry, but I have no choice. We're getting ready for church and Bible study group when I ask Mom about Claudine.

"I don't know, sweetheart." Mom stops brushing my hair. "Ms. Dimasalang and her daughter rarely visit the resort. It's usually Ms. Dimasalang's partner who's there."

I frown. "But don't they own the resort?"

"Yes, but other people run it for them."

It must be nice, being rich. There are people who'll do everything for you, including running your business. And my mother is one of those people who do things for them.

This leaves a bitter taste in my mouth.

Mom must read my expression, because she stops brushing my hair. "My sweet, darling honey Bee! Come here."

My mother hugs me, and I hug her back.

"You carry the world on your shoulders, and you're only

twelve," she murmurs into my hair. "Our life will get better, I promise you."

"It already is, Mom," I assure her. Yes, I'm very worried about Claudine. If something bad happened to her because of the gayuma, it's on me. And yes, I think it's really unfair that there are very few people who live with so much privilege while many do not. But I'm happy I have such a loving family. Knowing this makes me feel better, at least for bit.

The clock above the whiteboard reads three fifteen p.m.

Bible study has begun, but Claudine still isn't here. She's always on time.

Did something happen to her?

"Today we're having a special treat!" Mr. Bradbury announces as he pulls down the projector screen. "We're watching a cartoon of David and Goliath."

While our volunteer catechist discusses 1 Samuel 17, the story of David and Goliath, my imagination takes over.

I picture myself being the small David, taking on Goliath-Claudine, who makes the lives of Bible Study Town's residents miserable. But instead of going to battle, David-Jolina defeats the giant with smarts and a handful of gayuma-ed yema balls.

The animation ends with a slain Goliath and a victorious David. Then the screen fades to black.

Yikes.

Did I make Claudine sick? I didn't mean for that to happen. I just wanted Claudine to become a better person. Did I put anything bad in there?

Bad milk, maybe? But I was so sure about the condensed milk I took from the pantry. We cook so much for the canteen that food never stays around long enough to expire.

What if it was the potion itself? There was black smoke that smelled bad before it turned pink. Was that an omen? Or was something bad in the gayuma? Maybe I shouldn't have tried making such an advanced brew. I can't even make the beginner's brew right.

Then I remember the warning in the potion recipe, *follow the standard precautions.*

My stomach drops. I'm 100 percent sure I did all the protective prayers on the magic palayok before I began brewing the gayuma. Was there anything else I needed to do aside from the protective spells, the prayer, and being clear about my intentions?

One of the twins, Judy, passes me a coloring page of a cartoon David and Goliath. "You okay?"

"I'm fine," I mutter, dumping some crayons on my table. The twins don't frequently sit near me, so if they're noticing how antsy I am, I must be *that* obvious. I sigh. Might as well finish this coloring page.

"Magandang hapon, friends!"

I look up from my work and find Claudine wishing her

friends a good afternoon. I'm pretty sure I'm not included in that greeting—I'm usually not. But it's such a relief to see her. Best of all, she doesn't look sick or anything bad like that.

"Well, well, well!" Mr. Bradbury dusts off his fingers and tosses Claudine a yema ball from the bowl on his desk. "I thought we weren't seeing you today, Miss Dimasalang."

"Sorry, Mr. Bradbury." Claudine flashes the American catechist a grin. "I woke up late! I couldn't do this very important thing until last night, when we arrived from the mainland. Mom and I bought so much stuff for the party! Just let me know what I need to do and I will get on it." She doesn't even look at me.

I breathe a sigh of relief. Oh well. Apparently, I made another mess of a potion with the gayuma—just like the other potions I've tried to brew with Lolo Sebyo. Claudine is still her typical friendly-to-everyone-but-Jolina self.

Well, that is, until she plops into the seat next to me instead of her front-row middle seat.

I don't know what to think.

"Your seat's up there," I say carefully. I don't want to say anything that will set her off—Mr. Bradbury might throw us out of Bible study if we squabble.

"Nope. I'm sitting here. Mr. Bradbury doesn't have any rules about where we can sit, remember?" Claudine pops the yema ball into her mouth, placing her coloring page and crayons on the table.

"Yeah, but that's not where you usually sit." I frown. I always take the desk in the rightmost corner at the back of the room. Other kids usually sit around me, but having a table beside the back door makes me feel less enclosed. I get fresh air, and peace and quiet away from Claudine.

But now Claudine is sitting right beside me. I feel like I have no means of escape, even with the back door wide open. This is so weird. A thought gnaws at me. Is it possible that the gayuma actually worked?

"This is my new usual seat now." Claudine waves her hand, flipping her hair casually. I notice she has orange-and-gold highlights today. She turns her chair to face me. "So, Jolina. You're coming to my birthday, right? I'm not really good at using computers, so I had to stay up all night making your special invite!"

Claudine brandishes a white envelope and drops it on my table. I stare at it, waiting for it to jump or explode. "Is this some kind of a joke?"

"Nope. Definitely not a joke," Claudine chirps. She pushes the envelope closer to me. "Come on. Open it!"

I open the envelope with care, bringing out the invite as slowly as I would slice a slab of pork into bacon strips. Part of me expects a rubber snake to fall out of the envelope, or maybe something a lot grosser. I brace myself to see a mean drawing of me pop out. But to my surprise, it is what she said—an invitation to a party. Claudine's birthday party.

The invitation is full of pink glitter and hearts and stars.

There's even a rainbow unicorn printed in the middle. Above the tacky mythical horse are words loud and clear:

Hear ye! Hear ye!
Claudine Jessica Dimasalang is turning 12.
You are cordially invited to a feast celebrating
her special day!

Below the unicorn are the date and time, as well as the Dimasalangs' home address. On a separate card, Claudine printed:

To:
Jolina Bagayan and her cute doggo
Claudine Dimasalang's BFFAE
Please RSVP your attendance with
Claudine Dimasalang
(RSVP means let us know if you can come)

I blink once. Then twice. The words are still there. Claudine invited me to her birthday party, after publicly telling everyone she wasn't.

I can't believe the gayuma actually worked!

"This is very nice." I honestly don't know what else to say. "Um . . . thanks?"

Claudine beams.

"Kidlat is also invited?" I was just hoping to get an invite to her party. I didn't expect my dog would get one too. You know, I'm starting to like this gayuma thing.

"Oh, is that the cutie's name? Kidlat, as in 'lightning.' So very Filipino," Claudine says, nodding. "Of course he's invited. It's written there. I'd usually not invite a dog, but Kidlat seems to be very well behaved."

"He is. He's very special." I give her a smile. Anyone who compliments my dog deserves a smile, even a gayuma-ed mean girl like Claudine. I read the invitation again. "What's a BFFAE?"

"Duh. *Bee-ef-fay*. BFFAE." Claudine rolls her eyes. She puts the last crayon, the yellow one, in place. "Best Friend Forever And Ever."

Oh wow. No one has ever called me their best friend before. I know it's not real, but it still feels really good.

"So, you're coming, right?" Claudine reaches over my desk and arranges my crayons in rainbow order. "I can ask Sunshine to let you go, if you're worried about your mother. I just can't not have you there. My birthday won't be complete without you!"

Okay. This is starting to get weird.

"Everything all right there, kids?" Mr. Bradbury calls from his desk.

"Yes, Mr. Bradbury," Claudine and I answer at the same time.

Claudine moves back to her desk and pretends to color David and Goliath. She inches her chair closer to me, so close that I can smell her cotton candy–scented body spray. I've always wanted to buy one of those, but the only brand carrying that scent is too expensive for us.

"Well?" Claudine prompts under her breath. "Will you come?"

Claudine seems to really, *really* want me there. It's so weird. I feel like I've entered a totally different dimension where Mean Claudine is actually my friend.

But this isn't real, a voice in the back of my mind reminds me.

I shouldn't get used to this. It's only temporary. Soon, Claudine will be back to her old mean self. I feel bad (just a teeny-weeny bit) knowing that she probably has no idea why she's being so nice to me. But every time I remember Claudine constantly provoking and embarrassing me in front of everyone, I get a reassuring feeling that she totally deserves this.

"Of course I'll go." I give my new BFFAE a smile. "I wouldn't miss your birthday for anything."

CHAPTER ELEVEN

A Barrage of Clingy Text Messages

If my phone vibrates one more time, I'm going to chuck it out the classroom window. Claudine has been texting me nonstop.

The BFF thing is weird enough, but this incessant messaging is a whole new level of weirdness. I make a mental note to read up more on the potency of gayuma. Maybe I put too much in the candy, making Claudine so annoyingly clingy.

I would turn off my phone if not for Mom and Dad's rule never to do so. They want to be able to contact me easily in case of an emergency.

But at the rate Claudine is texting? My cheap secondhand phone is going to give up and shut itself down—and I won't blame it for doing so.

Ringgggggg!!!

The dismissal bell finally chimes, and I say good-bye to Marvin and Angelou and my other classmates. Thankfully, Marvin and Angelou wave back. My other classmates just nod or smile shyly at me.

I guess I still have my dayo vibe.

"Ack!"

My phone buzzes in my pocket again. It sends a jolt down my thigh, and I almost trip on the school's front steps. I groan as I bring the phone out of my school uniform's skirt pocket. "What now?"

I tap the screen. But instead of Claudine's name, I see Mom's. Phew!

Hi, honey Bee! Ms. Dimasalang's daughter is at the resort today. She asked about you. I gave her your number, but I told her you can't reply while in school. See you later. Love you lots!

Claudine obviously didn't take my mom's note seriously.

I let out an irritated sigh, finding Claudine's name and tapping it to load her message thread.

Oh wow. What a message thread!

Claudine asks me how I am, she tells me what she's doing, who she's doing what she's doing with—it's like she's sending me a text message every time she breathes in and sends another one whenever she breathes out. She sends a different text message for every single sentence. I guess that's how people text when they're not using a prepaid number, unlike me and my parents. They don't have to worry about running out of prepaid credits and having to top up.

I go through the long thread of Claudine's one-sentence messages. It's like getting a blow-by-blow account of her entire day.

My fingers freeze at the last message:

I can't wait to see you! ♥ ♥ ♥

Can't wait— What? I scroll up and stare at the message right above it:

I'm on my way. We're hanging out today, BFFAE!

My eyes widen. Claudine can't be serious, can she?

I elbow my way through the throngs of kids going out of the school gates, my eyes on the road. There are cars, jeepneys, and tricycles passing by. Some of them stop by the school, but none of them stop in front of me.

My heart sinks. Claudine was just messing with me. Even under the gayuma's magic, she's still messing with me.

I make my way to the waiting area, where kids are falling in line for tricycles. But before I can reach it, a white SUV pulls up beside me. Its window slides down, and out pops Claudine's face.

"Huy! San ka pupunta?" Claudine asks where I'm going. "I told you I'd pick you up!"

"Um . . ." I can't tell her that I'm finding it hard to believe she would really go out of her way to see me without going into the gayuma thing, so I just keep my mouth shut.

"Why didn't you text me back?" Claudine pouts. "Sunshine said you'd reply."

I wince at Claudine's calling of my mom by her first name. Even gayuma-ed, Claudine is still disrespectful.

"I was in class. You know that we're not allowed to use our phones in class," I say, keeping my tone even. "I was going to say I can't go. My dog . . . he's waiting for me at Nanay Dadang's. We always walk home together. And I haven't asked my parents for permission. I can't just leave."

"We'll pick up your dog." Claudine says this like it's the most obvious thing in the world. She opens the door. "Get in. We're hanging out. I already asked Sunshine if you could come, and she said yes."

"She didn't say—"

Buzzzzzttt! My phone vibrates again with another message from Mom.

So nice of Claudine to surprise you. Be home by five— you still have school tomorrow. Have fun at the port! Love you loads.

I peek inside Claudine's family's car. I can smell the leather of the pristine white seats. Never mind the fact that Claudine is surprisingly okay with having my muddy dog join us there. I'm not comfortable with the idea that Claudine is making plans for me without even considering whether I want to.

My irritation worsens as I think about Mom more. Did

Claudine order my mother to let us hang out on a school day? It's so unlike Mom to say yes to something like that.

"Stop calling my mom by her first name," I say in a firm, even way. I feel the gayuma's magic flow with my words. "I don't like it when you do."

"Okay." Claudine blinks. Then she offers her hand. "Well? Are you coming?"

I look at my classmates in the long line for tricycles that will take them home. I look at other students walking in groups by the side of the road. I look at Claudine, alone in the back seat, comfortable in her roomy, air-conditioned SUV.

Hang out? Sure. We'll hang out. But not in the way she expects.

I take Claudine's hand and climb up into the SUV beside her.

CHAPTER TWELVE
The Broken Fish

After picking up Kidlat at Nanay Dadang's, Claudine's driver drops us off at the public market beside the Isla Pag-Ibig port. A weird combination of smells whiff under my nose—tricycle exhaust, frying fish balls, and salt water from the sea.

I enjoy going to the palengke, the marketplace, whenever I run errands for Lolo, or when I'm accompanying Dad to buy ingredients for the eatery. There are three main buildings—the wet, seafood, and dry markets. The wet market is where vendors sell pork, beef, poultry, and even goat or carabao meat. The seafood market, as the name implies, is where the seafood and fish vendors are. The vendors in the dry market aren't just selling fruits, veggies, and condiments though. They also offer a wide variety of "dry" products such as random kitchenware and even everyday clothes.

Like this pretty blue-and-green flower blouse that catches my eye.

"Bili na." The vendor encourages me to buy.

I look at the cardboard label hanging over the blouses. Two hundred pesos. It's too expensive for me, but maybe not for Claudine.

An idea pops into my head.

"What do you think?" I say, holding the blouse over my chest.

WOOF! Kidlat runs around in a circle, excited.

"I suppose that means I'll look good in it," I say, grinning.

"He's right." Claudine comes up to me, straightening the blouse's sleeve. "You know, I didn't think much of it on the hanger, but it actually looks good on you."

"I know." I sigh dramatically, putting the blouse back on the rack. I tell the vendor I'll just get it next time, as my money isn't enough. "Next time na lang po. Kulang pera ko eh."

I peer at Claudine out of the corner of my eye while I do a mental chant: *Buy it for me. Come on, Claudine. Offer to buy it for me.*

I feel the magic of my command, the suggestion of my mentally spoken words making its way to Claudine. Let's see how badly she wants to be my BFF.

"I'll buy it for you," she says, taking the blouse off the rack again. "If you really want it, that is."

"Really?" Wow.

"Ate, we'll get the blouse po," Claudine says, referring to

the woman as "older sister" as she brings out a thousand-peso bill from her wallet. Funny how she can refer to strangers with an honorific while she calls my mom by her first name. "Sorry, wala po kong barya eh."

Claudine doesn't have smaller bills. And to think the only time I ever owned a thousand-peso bill was when one of my richer godparents visited us in Marikina for Christmas. He wanted to make up three years' worth of gifts to me with the bill.

I don't know why, but this makes me even more irritated with Claudine. She has everything so easy.

Well, I'm not going to make this easy for her. I take the pretty blouse without remorse. This isn't taking advantage—this is payback.

I look around the port for ideas. There's a wedding reception going on at a restaurant near the docks. I figure that might be a good place to start having some fun. Well, that is, until I see the happy couple kiss and toast with their family and friends.

Scratch that. No need to ruin those people's special day. Claudine's the one who was awful to me, not them.

I just want Claudine to know how it felt to be embarrassed the same way she made me feel that day in Bible study when she told everyone she wouldn't be inviting me.

But how?

My gaze falls on the seafood market across the street. Aha!

"Let's go there," I say. The seafood market stands near the docks, where fishermen from all over the island trade their freshest catch of the day. "Freshest" means that the fish and seafood came straight from the sea, and most often it's still alive.

This should be interesting.

Claudine frowns. She points to the coffee shop beside the restaurant. "Don't you want to have iced chocolate first? My treat. Tita Sunshine said you always get one when you're here."

That's true. Iced chocolate is one of my favorite drinks. I always make sure to get a cup every time I'm buying stuff for Lolo or accompanying Dad. But now isn't the time for iced chocolate. I have more important things to do . . . like give Claudine a taste of her own medicine.

I cross the street with Claudine in tow, weaving through the seafood market I'm so familiar with while keeping an eye on her. It's pretty obvious she's never explored this part of the docks—her eyes are darting from one stall to another. From the trays of prepared squid to the live shrimp swimming in multicolored plastic basins spread out on the stall tables, Claudine is drinking everything in. She wrinkles her nose now and then, as if trying to hide her disgust at the smell of fish and seafood peddled by fishermen.

We round the corner, and I find the stall I'm looking for. It's the stall selling fresh hito—slimy, slithering, and breathing catfish in a shallow tray of water. "Have you ever touched a hito?"

"No," Claudine answers with a grimace. "I've never touched a live fish before."

"Any fish?"

Claudine shrugs.

"Wow. You've lived all your life on an island, and yet you've never touched a live fish?" I shake my head. "Have you at least eaten a hito?"

"Duh." Claudine rolls her eyes. "Fried hito is my favorite. It's not just poor people food, you know."

Seriously? *Poor people food?* This girl is so rude.

"Touch it," I say.

"Touch what?"

"The hito." I point to the tray of fish. "Just touch it with one little finger."

"Why?"

"Think of it as your BFFAE initiation," I explain. This is interesting. She didn't blink an eye when I wished for her to buy me a blouse, but she's hesitating to touch a fish. "It's hard to be friends with somebody who's never even touched a live fish."

"What's that have to do with being friends?"

Nothing. Absolutely nothing.

"Just touch it," I order. I invoke the magic of the arbularyo, let my power come coursing through my words.

Claudine touches the fish. "It's slimy. And it's . . . hmmm . . . it's actually not so bad— *Eek!*"

The fish slithers away without warning, and Claudine accidentally touches all the other fish. This surprises the other fish, which in turn surprises more fish. Now all the fish are agitated.

In the commotion, the hito vendor arrives. "What's going on? Why are the fish—"

"EEK!"

Claudine, the vendor, and I shriek as a hito jumps out of the tray and onto the ground. The fish tries to make its way to me but can't as Kidlat blocks its path. Fast as lightning, my dog grabs the fish with his mouth.

"Good boy, Kidlat!" I say. Claudine cheers.

Kidlat drops the fish in front of me. He must have bit it too hard, because it's no longer moving.

Oh no. My dog has broken the fish!

"I'm so sorry, ate," I tell the vendor, bringing out my wallet. I only have one hundred pesos, which was supposed to last me a few more days. But the dead fish is my fault. "This is all I have—"

"I got this." Claudine pushes my hand away. She gives the vendor five hundred pesos. "We'll also buy some hito. It might be better if you pick the fish though."

"I sure will," the vendor snaps, but she takes Claudine's money anyway and even selects the best fish for her.

Leave it to Claudine to fix everything with money. But

I can't complain—this is definitely better than getting into trouble.

Claudine skips as she carries her bag of hito. "That was fun! It's the first time I've ever bought hito."

It wasn't supposed to be fun—not for her anyway. But since we're here already, we go around the seafood market for a bit. By around four thirty, Claudine has bought clams, shrimp, mussels, and lato.

"What are you going to do with all that seafood?" I ask. I can think of so many ways to cook it. Boiled in soda and ginger. Sautéed in butter, garlic, and sugar. Baked with garlic, olive oil, and a huge amount of gooey melted cheese. I'd be able to do a lot of things with the seafood—if only I could afford it.

"Well, I plan to eat it," Claudine says, grinning.

"Obviously."

I meet her playful gaze and burst out laughing. Claudine joins me but ends up in a coughing fit. I thump her on the back, but the smile hasn't left my face.

We're eating taho—a soybean curd with tapioca balls and brown sugar syrup—by the docks while waiting for Claudine's driver to pick us up. Claudine's the one who paid for the taho, of course.

"We should do this again," she says, downing the last of the tapioca balls in her cup.

I don't answer immediately.

There were times during the afternoon when it wasn't

that painful being with Claudine. It's usually when she's not talking. But the moment she opens her mouth, Claudine says things that hurt me. I don't even know if she's aware of it. So I'm not sure if hanging out too often is a good idea.

But that doesn't mean I won't make the most of it.

"I'd like to, but I can't," I tell her. Maybe I can get a tad bit more out of this spell. "I need to help Dad at the carinderia. Lolo Sebyo helps with the customers, but he's useless in the kitchen."

"What about your mom?"

It's exactly the question I'm waiting for.

"She's not a regular employee yet at your resort, so she has to work overtime to earn enough money for our family. But that also means she can't help out at the eatery, so I have to do it. Unless you could *ask your mom to speed up Mom's promotion*?" I hold my breath.

Without hesitation, Claudine nods. "I got this." She pats my hand. "I'll make sure my BFFAE is well taken care of. Nothing is ever going to come between us."

I can't say I feel the same way. But if it means getting Mom promoted, then suffering through the irritating clinginess of this girl is well worth it.

CHAPTER THIRTEEN

Claudine Dimasalang at Your Service

School used to be a chore, but now I'm grateful for it. It's the best excuse I can give Claudine to get her out of my hair.

Claudine kept bugging me about hanging out during the school week. Being homeschooled, it's hard for her to understand why I just can't go out whenever I feel like it.

But as her birthday drew near, it was harder to tell her off. She's just too excited.

I tried to invoke the magic through a text message and a phone call. I can't think my demands remotely either. As it turns out, invoking gayuma magic can only be done when I'm physically present around Claudine.

I understand that Lolo Sebyo's gayuma book wouldn't have anything about texting and phone calls, since it was published in the early 1900s. But it should have at least mentioned that thinking demands remotely doesn't work either. The book is pretty much useless.

Needless to say, it's been a long week.

Finally—thankfully—it's Saturday.

"Okay, sweetheart, let's try this again." Mom takes me by the shoulders. "Remember—"

"Don't talk unless Ms. Dimasalang asks a question. Be sure to keep Kidlat out of trouble." I sigh. We've been through this four times already. "I know, Mom."

Ever since I told her Kidlat and I were invited to Claudine's party, Mom has been so happy. She's always urging me to make friends in Isla Pag-Ibig. I wasn't sure how she'd feel about me missing a potions lesson, but she said it wouldn't hurt to miss just one.

I take a deep breath, trying to calm my racing heart. Mom's concern is contagious. She's oozing so much worry, and I'm absorbing it all like a kitchen sponge.

Honestly, my mother has nothing to worry about. Ms. Dimasalang probably won't even notice I'm there. But I get it. It was very difficult for Mom to find a job on the island, and she felt lucky to land the one she did. The Dimasalangs' resort, the Sampaguita Premiere Villas, is the biggest resort on Isla Pag-Ibig, and everyone wants to work there. I just hope Claudine follows through with getting Mom promoted from being a trainee to a regular employee.

Something wet and warm touches my hand—it's Kidlat.

He has already jumped out of our tricycle and is waiting for me. Seeing my dog instantly calms me down.

As long as Kidlat is with me, I'm going to be okay.

"Honey, she'll be fine," Dad says as he adjusts his cap. He kicks the pedal of the motorcycle attached to the tricycle. The engine roars to life. "J-Bee is a good kid. I'm sure your boss will like her."

"You can come with me if you want," I suggest. I don't really like the idea of having my mom hang around an obviously for-kids party. But if it's going to make her feel better, why not? "Claudine invited you too, you know."

"Dad's right. *Again*." Mom rolls her eyes. She gives me a kiss on the forehead. "Nah. I don't need to be there. Enjoy. Dad will pick you up after dinner. Oh, gosh. I'm so happy you're finally making friends!"

"I will." I'm trying to act calm for my mother, but I wish she'd have a little more faith in me.

As the Dimasalangs' mansion looms above the tall, heavy gates, it dawns on me. My family and I might be happy we have one another, but one thing's clear: We're poor and the Dimasalangs are not.

"Good afternoon," greets the Dimasalangs' security guard. Yep, they have their own security guard. Whereas at our canteen, Kidlat is the nearest thing we have for security. Maybe it's just my imagination, but I think I see the guard's jaw twitch at the sight of Lolo's beat-up tricycle. "Miss Claudine is waiting for you inside."

I tighten my grip on Kidlat's leash as I wave goodbye to my parents.

"Just go straight up the path," the guard says, pointing to a long driveway flanked by coconut trees and rows of blue flowers. It leads straight to a covered area in front of a modern mansion. Then the man goes back to the guardhouse by the gate.

I'm on my own.

Halfway up the driveway, Kidlat and I see a figure running toward us. Claudine.

"You're here!" She throws her arms around my neck. "And you're wearing the blouse I bought you! But you're also late. I've been waiting all day."

"But your invitation says two o'clock—"

"Never mind. You're here, and that's what matters." Claudine beams. She leans down toward Kidlat.

"Wait! He's not used to strangers—" But to my surprise, Kidlat allows Claudine to pat him. Hmm. If Kidlat likes her, maybe Claudine isn't so bad after all. I give Claudine my birthday gift. It's a bag full of Bagayan's Best Yema Balls—without gayuma. "I made these for you. Happy birthday!"

"Oh. Thank you!" Claudine's face lights up as I hand her the gift. Without hesitation, she takes a yema ball and rips the wrapper off. "Mmmm! This is so good. No one's ever made me yema balls before."

"Your mom doesn't cook?" I ask.

"Mommy is too busy with work." Claudine shakes her head. "We have a great cook though! She just doesn't know how to make yema balls."

My own mother doesn't know how to cook, but Lola Toyang and Dad do. I mean, I live with a family of cooks, so it's kind of hard to imagine not having anyone who can make you yema balls or teach you how to make them.

"Come on, I'll show you around." Claudine drags me inside the house and into the parlor. Or what I think is the parlor. It looks more like a cathedral to me. There are two huge winding staircases leading to two doors. I half expect a princess to come down from one side and her beast boyfriend on the other.

"We'll see my room later." Claudine pulls me to the big double doors underneath the stairway balcony. "For now, we eat!"

The door opens to a huge ballroom with floor-to-ceiling windows. Even from where we stand, I can see the waters of San Bernardino Strait and the clear blue sky.

It's so pretty that I almost forget why I'm here in the first place—to make this girl pay for all the mean things she did to me.

When we reach the buffet table, I notice something isn't

right. There isn't any food in the serving dishes. The table decorations aren't even done yet. All I can see is a tray of baked macaroni, a small basket of garlic bread, and a pitcher of iced tea good enough for two people.

I swallow hard as the knot in my stomach tightens. "Where is everyone?"

It's all been some kind of prank. The gayuma didn't work after all. Claudine is still her mean self.

"They're not here yet, silly." Claudine giggles.

The sound grates on my nerves. If she thinks I'm not smart enough to figure out this trick she's playing, she's totally mistaken. I turn to leave. "Let's go, Kidlat!"

"What? Why? No, don't go. I'm not playing a trick on you, if that's what you're thinking," Claudine insists. She puts a hand on my arm. "Please. People won't be arriving until dinner. I invited you early so we could have some time alone together. I'm telling you the truth, I swear."

I stare at Claudine, the girl who's been making my life difficult in this province since I arrived. She has this begging look on her face that reminds me of Kidlat whenever he wants a treat.

The gayuma is still at work—and she's being genuine.

"I don't drink iced tea," I say slowly. It's amazing how well the gayuma works. I can't believe I really managed to pull this off. "I'd like an orange juice instead. Or maybe just cold water?"

"Stay here. Sit down. Don't leave, okay?" In a flash, Claudine's gone.

I sit at the empty table, watching Kidlat sniff around.

"What do you think, good boy?" I ask my dog. "Wouldn't it be nice to have a home as big as this?"

Kidlat looks at me and sneezes. I guess it's a no.

I laugh. "Okay. Well, we have the entire day to live like rich people. Come here, have some macaroni."

I'm feeding Kidlat on a paper plate when Claudine arrives.

"Ta-da!" She brandishes two pitchers, one full of fresh orange juice and the other full of ice-cold water. "I tried to make the orange juice myself, but it tasted gross, so I had Ate Rica make it."

"Thanks." I watch Claudine pour a water and an orange juice for both of us. Wow. The gayuma really is working well.

While we eat, Claudine won't stop talking. "Mommy ordered the international menu from the caterer. I'd prefer if we had some of the stuff your canteen serves, but Mommy won't have any of it." Claudine rolls her eyes. "Her friends and their kids aren't used to Filipino cuisine, she says."

"Mm-hmm . . ." I mumble, showing her that I'm listening even as I stuff myself with baked macaroni.

"I wouldn't invite them if not for Mommy," she continues. Claudine toys with her fork. "But at least I'll have guests. I'm not sure if the kids from Sunday school will come."

Hmm. This is new. I've always thought Claudine was this popular, snotty rich girl. Now I wonder whether she has any friends at all. A tiny part of me feels bad for her.

"They'll come," I assure her. But honestly? I don't really know for sure. I mean, I always assumed she had tons of friends, but maybe she only sees them in Bible class. Maybe they'll come, but maybe they won't. Either way, that's something she doesn't have to hear. She seems to be stressed enough as it is.

"Are you done?" Claudine asks as I swallow the last of the baked macaroni on my plate. "There's someone I want you to meet."

I was actually hoping to get another serving, but I'm curious. Claudine looks really excited for me to meet whoever that is. "Who?"

Claudine winks. "You'll see."

CHAPTER FOURTEEN
Dogs Rule, Cats Drool!

I didn't know who to expect, but I definitely never thought that the "someone" Claudine wanted me to meet wouldn't be a person at all—it's a cat. Claudine's old pet cat.

"Thanks, Ate Rica," she says, taking the very furry, all-white cat from one of their maids. The woman returns Claudine's smile before leaving. "This is Winter. Winter is my best friend. I've had her since I was born."

"Hi, Winter." I pat the cat on the head, tightening my grip on Kidlat's leash. I snapped on his leash the moment I saw Ate Rica carry Claudine's cat. What in the world is Claudine thinking, making me bring my *dog* to meet her *cat*? Cats and dogs can't be friends.

As expected, Winter the cat hisses at Kidlat. But my dog, being the good dog he is, sits at attention in front of her, his tail wagging gently. He doesn't flinch. He doesn't even blink when she threatens him with her paw. Winter's claws are surprisingly retracted. It's like she's testing how Kidlat's going to react. Kind of trying to see how far his patience will go.

Kidlat sits calmly beside me for a good five minutes just watching the cat, while Claudine and I talk. And just like that, Winter is lying on her back with her legs in the air, inviting Kidlat to play.

"Your dog is amazing," Claudine says, smiling widely. "Every dog Winter meets ends up fighting with her. But Kidlat didn't even flinch! I knew he'd behave."

"Who's a good boy?" I reward Kidlat with a belly rub. "You are!"

"You should let him roam without a leash," Claudine suggests.

"Nah." I shake my head. "It's his first time here and he's just met her. I have to keep him on a leash until they're truly BFFs. Just to be safe."

"Good point." Claudine grins. Maybe it's because I always see her scowling around me, but it's only now that I notice she has a dimple on her right cheek. "They'll be BFFs like us in no time!"

"Right." I hide my snort with a cough. This gayuma-ed Claudine actually seems like a nice person. But it's not easy to forget months of meanness from this girl. Besides, no one's ever reached BFF status with me. Except Kidlat.

Because to be a best friend and have a best friend means you let people get really close to you. Even my *close* friends in Manila didn't really know all of me. I never told them that the Bagayans practice magic. No one knows the real me aside from my family.

Claudine carries her cat on her shoulder as she shows me around her house. Though I really can't call the Dimasalang house a "house." It really is a mansion. A sprawling, gigantic mansion. I could put five of Lolo Sebyo's house inside and there'd still be room to spare. There are so many doors and hallways. I'd totally end up falling into the sea if I entered the wrong one.

One thing I notice though . . . There seem to be no photos of Claudine's dad. It's always Claudine and her mom, or her mom with people who look a lot like her. They all have Claudine's deep-set eyes and high-bridged nose.

"They're Mommy's siblings," Claudine explains. "Some of them are dead, but most of them are living in Manila."

It never ceases to amaze me how Claudine can be so blunt, even when talking about her own family.

I know it's not my place to ask, and she'd probably answer anything because of the gayuma, but I'm curious. Besides, if she does something awful to me again when the gayuma wears off, I'll have some dirt on her. Am I being mean? I guess. But the past months being her punching bag haven't been easy, you know. "Which one is your dad?"

Claudine winces. "We don't have a picture of him."

"Oh." I blink. Okay, I take it back. I *am* being too mean. "I'm sorry."

"It's okay. This is Mommy, in case you haven't figured it out yet." Claudine points to a picture. Claudine's mom is as pretty as her. She seems older than my mom, but still very beautiful. Ms. Dimasalang actually reminds me of those rare morena actresses starring in the Tagalog movies Mom loves to watch. The media prefers light-skinned actresses, so it's not often I see someone with dark brown skin get the spotlight.

"I never met my father. Mommy said he had another family. They didn't want a scandal, so they gave Mommy a lot of money to keep quiet." Claudine pauses, shifting her sleeping cat to her other shoulder. "Mommy is so hardworking. She raised me on her own and built this house for us and runs the best resort on the island."

"It's not just hard work." As much as I don't want to jeopardize Mom's job, I just can't help myself. It doesn't sit right with me not to speak up. "My parents are hardworking too, but they don't have a truckload of money to start their own resort. And because of that, they might never be able to have such a successful business. Not because they're lazy, but it's just the way the world works, you know? It's just . . . It's just—"

"Unfair," Claudine finishes for me. She nods soberly.

"Yeah."

We continue the house tour in silence. I feel terrible saying those things to Claudine on her birthday, but she needs to know how lucky she is.

The picture frames on the walls change as we walk farther down the hallway. I notice a woman with long black hair appear often in photos with Claudine and her mom. The woman looks to be Mom's age, and her hair is so thick and long and layered that it reminds me of a black bird's feathers. "Who's this lady? She's very pretty."

"She's Raven," Claudine answers. I notice a change in her tone. She sounds wary. "She's my mom's partner."

"Business partner?"

"No." Claudine shakes her head. "Life partner."

I feel Claudine's eyes on me, like she's testing me or something. But I understand. Many people in our country aren't very welcoming to relationships like Ms. Dimasalang and Raven's. I see nothing wrong with it though. If anything, Claudine should be proud of her family. Love is love.

"Your mom sounds amazing," I say. And I mean it. Her mother does sound like a superwoman.

"She is." Claudine opens the door to a room with mint-green walls. Winter the cat jumps off her shoulder, sauntering to her cat mansion beside the queen-sized bed. "Welcome to my abode!"

Everything in Claudine's bedroom seems like it was cut precisely and fitted like a jigsaw puzzle. All her things are also properly labeled. Her dolls' clothes are arranged according to season: winter, spring, summer, fall. There's even a "rainy" season. Claudine is so weird.

But the thing I'm drawn to the most is the beautiful bike parked on one side of the room.

"It's nice, isn't it?" Claudine takes the bike off the stand. "Mommy got it for me from Manila. Do you have a bike?"

I frown. I really don't like talking to anyone about what happened to my family, most especially to Claudine. But she did tell me her story, so it's only fair that I tell her mine.

"I used to. But we had to sell it to help pay for my grandmother's cancer treatment," I say, kneeling to turn the pedal with my hand. The chains are well oiled and clean, like it hasn't been used yet. "My bike had a basket too so Kidlat could ride with me."

"That sounds fun," Claudine says wistfully. "Would you and Kidlat ride with me if you had a bike?"

"Sure." I mean it, really. Last week, Claudine would have been the last person I'd go riding with. But now? I don't know.

It's odd, and I didn't think I'd ever say this, but Claudine and I are more similar than I initially thought. We enjoy the same things. If our circumstances were different, would we have been friends? Like, *real friends*, not the gayuma-induced kind. If my mom didn't work for her family, would she have hung out with me? If I didn't have dark gums, if I had more money, would she have considered me a friend?

"Awesome." Claudine smiles. "Come by the window. Let's take a picture with Winter and Kidlat."

We take a picture. And another one. And another. Both our phones are full of our faces by the time we're through.

"Your dog really knows how to pose!" Claudine laughs. "Look at him. That head tilt!"

"I know, right?" I point at Winter. The scowling cat looks like her face was smooshed on a glass window. "But your cat doesn't seem to like selfies. She looks so grouchy."

Claudine giggles. "She's always grouchy."

I join her in laughter.

Real or not, it's nice to laugh with a friend.

"Claudine!" A shrill voice calls from outside Claudine's bedroom. "Where is that girl? CLAUDINE!"

"That's Mommy." Claudine's laughter dies down, and she sighs loudly. "I'm in my room!"

Ms. Dimasalang appears in the doorway. "What are you doing here— Oh, hello."

"This is Jolina. She's Sun—" Claudine throws me a wary look, as though afraid I'll be mad at her. "I mean, she's my friend."

I don't like the idea of anyone fearing me. But I do appreciate that she didn't call my mom by her first name. One thing though. I'm torn about letting Ms. Dimasalang know that my mother works for her. Part of me wants to tell her who I am, thinking that maybe it'll put Mom in her good graces at work. Another part of me doesn't want to—the same part of me that feels weird about this whole thing. My parents told me that not being rich is okay, but I don't know. It's just awkward.

"You remind me of someone." Ms. Dimasalang peers at me. I feel like I'm under a microscope with her scrutiny. "What's your surname?"

One of the things I've noticed about living in a small province like Isla Pag-Ibig is the importance of surnames. The community is small enough that everyone knows everyone else, growing up together, generation by generation. Some are more powerful and prominent than others.

We're far from a "powerful" family, but my grandfather is known by everyone. Ms. Dimasalang will certainly recognize our surname. There's no point in hiding it.

"Bagayan po, Ms. Dimasalang," I say. "I'm Sunshine and Rainier Bagayan's daughter. Sebyo Bagayan is my grandfather."

"Oh! No wonder you look so familiar." Recognition dawns on Ms. Dimasalang's face. "Call me Tita Peachy. How is your grandfather? I see him at church, but I've always wanted to visit his eatery. Do you still sell the yema balls? I loved them as a child! Where is your mother? Claudine, why didn't you invite Sunshine?"

"*Mom-myyyy!*" Claudine groans. "Stop it, please. You're embarrassing me! Why are you looking for me anyway?"

"Oh yes!" Tita Peachy nods. "You distracted me, silly girl. Your guests are here. I'll see you downstairs?"

"Yes, yes." Claudine pushes her mother to the door. "I just need to change first."

"Why? Your dress is fine!"

"Mommyyy!"

"Okay. Okay!" Tita Peachy holds her hands up in surrender. "See you downstairs."

"Ugh. My mom is so makulit." Claudine rolls her eyes, meaning that her mother is annoying.

"I think she's nice." I'm not just saying that to make Claudine feel better. Ms. Dimasalang—or Tita Peachy, she prefers to be called—is nicer than I expected. She's not the snobby rich lady I imagined. "And I agree with her. You look great in that dress already."

"Really?"

"Really." Again, I'm telling the truth. Claudine really does look pretty. Her yellow sundress with teal, green, and purple reminds me of the beach—its bright colors make a pretty contrast to her brown skin.

"Okay. I'll stick to it, then." Claudine grins, flipping her hair. I notice she doesn't have any colorful streaks today. "Let's go downstairs before Mommy comes back."

Claudine hoists grumpy old Winter on her shoulder before stepping out of the room. Maybe Claudine isn't that bad a person. After all, anyone who likes animals and can actually have animals like them is usually a good person.

CHAPTER FIFTEEN

Happy Birthday, Claudine

It's amazing what a huge difference a few hours can make. The ballroom has turned into a fairy-tale land.

Above us, there are giant paper cutouts in three different shades of green hanging from the ceiling. There are yellow Christmas lights in jars in the middle of the dining tables. They remind me of little fairies trapped in jars in a magical forest.

"Have some roast beef, Kidlat," I say, putting a small piece in the dog's bowl on the chair beside me. Claudine lent him one of Winter's gazillion food bowls. "It's really good."

My dog eats the roast beef eagerly. I know how he feels. I'm happily stuffing myself, away from the people but close to the buffet table. We're all alone here with Winter, and I'm perfectly fine with it.

"What's up, Winter?" I check on the cat. She just looks at me and yawns.

I laugh. "You and me both."

Claudine is busy greeting her guests, but I don't mind not talking to anyone human. I don't know any of the guests anyway.

"You three doing okay?" Claudine stops by our table as I'm helping myself to a heaping spoonful of potato salad. "I swear I'll be with you soon. My guests—"

I swallow my food, waving a spoon at her. "Don't mind us. We're fine here. The food's wonderful, by the way."

"Awesome." Claudine is all smiles. "You should try the hazelnut shake. It's the best. I'll be back soon!"

And with that, we're alone again. Well, for a couple of minutes at least.

Two girls sit down across from me and the animals. They seem like they're my age, but I can't tell for sure. They're wearing makeup and designer clothes that make them look older.

"Are you Claudine's new Antonette?" the taller one, a white girl with light brown hair and hazel eyes, asks me. I can't know for sure if her eye color is real or fake. It's hard to know with foreigners.

"Am I Claudine's what?"

"Antonette," says the other one. She's a pretty Chinese Filipino girl with fair skin and full red lips. "Antonette is Claudine's best friend. She lives in the US now."

Before I can say anything, the tall white girl brandishes her fork like a baton and grins. "She *is* the new Antonette!"

"I'm Jolina." What a weirdo. "This is Kidlat—"

The girl flips her hair, Claudine style but with a lot more poise. "Selena Ciervo."

I don't really need to know her surname. But I guess if you're a Ciervo and you're on Isla Pag-Ibig, you make sure everyone knows who you are. Unlike Tita Peachy recognizing my family name, it's a different case with this Selena girl. The Ciervos were the first Spanish family to settle in Isla Pag-Ibig. Lolo Sebyo said they own almost a third of the land, a gift granted to their ancestors by the Spanish government when the Philippines was still a colony. Even now, a lot of their relatives have positions in government.

"I'm Maui. Hi, Kidlat!" the other girl chirps. "He's a cute dog."

"He is." I smile. Maui seems nicer than her friend.

Selena peers at Kidlat. "Jack Russell terriers are expensive. I've seen one cost as much as eighty thousand pesos. Are you rich?"

Okay. That's weird.

"No. A neighbor gave him to me as a gift." I don't really owe her any explanation. But I feel like she's going to assume I stole Kidlat if I don't tell her the truth.

"Oh."

Now I'm getting annoyed. What's this girl's problem?

I can't resist a jab of my own. "Is your mother a fan of Selena Gomez? You know, the singer?"

Selena's eyes narrow. "I'm named after my grandmother. My *Spanish* grandmother." She looks me up and down. "No. You can't be an Antonette. Antonette never wears cheap shirts and shorts. And your sneakers, what are those? I've never seen a Nike check mark so big!"

Selena giggles. Maui's smile looks pained.

I already know I don't belong here. Selena doesn't need to remind me of that.

I eat my food in silence, hoping the girls will leave me alone. Thankfully, Selena and Maui forget about me and talk about the fancy parties they attend with their international-school classmates in Manila. They talk about which European countries their parents will fly them to for summer break. Or which cruises they'll take. They talk about themselves, basically. But when Selena says going to Isla Pag-Ibig is not worth it anymore now that Antonette lives in the United States, it's time to butt in.

"Isn't Claudine your friend too?" Surely, attending her birthday party makes it worth visiting Isla Pag-Ibig. I can't help but feel bad for Claudine. If this is the type of person she's friends with, it's not surprising she says the mean things she does.

Maui toys with her fork. "Well, yeah. But—"

"Now I'm pretty sure you're new here. You have no idea." Selena's lips curl into a sneer. "Let me explain. Maui,

Antonette, and I . . . our families have been on this island for ages. Claudine's family—they're new blood. Peachy Dimasalang used to be this poor labandera who had Claudine with a rich married man. The man's family gave Peachy a lot of money, which she used to get rich herself."

A frown creases my forehead. Selena's telling of Claudine's family history is similar to what Claudine told me earlier, but it rubs me the wrong way. It's like she's mocking Tita Peachy. No wonder Claudine was embarrassed to tell me.

And honestly? Hearing her refer to Tita Peachy by just her first name grates on my ears.

"Ms. Dimasalang worked hard to get Sampaguita Premiere Villas where it is." I grit my teeth. This girl is really testing my patience. Maybe even more than Claudine ever did. "That's what my mom says."

"How does your mom know?" Selena raises a perfectly arched brow. I didn't know kids my age already got their eyebrows fixed.

"She works for Claudine's mom," I say, making sure to meet her gaze. I'm not ashamed of what my mom does. She's hardworking and she does everything she can to help my dad and Lolo Sebyo provide for our family. "She's a receptionist."

"Really? Fascinating."

Selena and Maui erupt in giggles. The sound reminds me of a hyena's cackle.

I ball my fists under the table. Kidlat licks the one nearest him, and his touch calms me down a bit. But just when I think of a witty and less-rude comeback, Claudine arrives at our table.

"Oh good!" she says. "You're getting to know each other."

Selena smirks. "We are. A whole lot."

A deafening silence falls on our table. I can feel the tension among the four of us humans. It's like the heat coming off an empty pan on an open stove—slowly smoldering before finally emitting a burnt smell and nasty smoke.

Maui clears her throat. "Is your mom doing an outreach program for your birthday, Claudine?"

Claudine and I exchange glances. What does she mean?

Then we follow Maui's gaze. My eyes land on new guests arriving—the kids from our Bible study group.

Is this girl for real? "Actually—" I begin.

"I got this." Claudine folds her table napkin and daintily dabs her lips. "No, they're my friends from Sunday school. Just like Jolina here."

Maui blinks. "Oh. I'm sorry, I didn't know—"

"It's okay. Excuse us, ladies. I have guests to entertain!" And with that, Claudine slams the napkin on the table, gathers her cat, and marches to where the Bible study kids are.

Personally, I think that Maui girl genuinely thought the kids were attending an outreach program. For one, it seems like something Tita Peachy would do. For another, the kids are dressed like me—simple jeans and shirts and sneakers screaming, *We are not rich like you!* Maui isn't a total snob like Selena. She's just really clueless.

I was expecting that Claudine would entertain the group as she said she would. But she stops and hides behind me instead. Which is pretty useless, as Claudine is a head taller than me. When I turn to face her, I notice she has tears in her eyes.

"I can't believe they came!" Claudine says, her voice breaking.

"Of course they came," I say. "Go show them the buffet table. Kidlat and I will help Tita Raven set up the videoke machine."

Tita Raven already has most of the wires sorted out when I reach her. "You must be Jolina." She has a really pretty smile. "Claudine told us so much about you. Is that Kidlat?"

When he hears his name, Kidlat hops up and takes a seat on the chair next to the one where I dumped my backpack.

I nod. "Yes po."

"He's as gorgeous as Claudine described! And so well behaved too. Please hold this." Tita Raven hands me the plug as she rummages behind the videoke machine. I hand it back to her outstretched hand. "It's so nice to see Claudine being friends with someone who loves animals as much as she does."

"Yeah." I say nothing more. I don't want to rag on Claudine's so-called friends, but I figure I don't need to. Tita Raven already knows.

"Claudine also told me about your mother's employment status at the resort," Tita Raven says. She gives me another pretty smile. "Sunshine's our best trainee, so you can be assured she'll be promoted soon."

Soon? Why can't they promote Mom now?

But of course I can't ask that, so I just thank her. "Salamat po."

It's better than nothing, I guess.

"Mic test. Test mic," Tita Raven speaks to the microphone. She adjusts the volume and repeats the process until she's satisfied. Tita Raven then hands the microphone to me, her hand poised on the keypad. "What song number?"

I take a step back. "I'm not singing. Claudine is."

"What? No!" Claudine makes herself comfortable on the chair beside Kidlat. Still, she takes the microphone from me. "You sing."

"Aw, come on. Sing for me, Claudine." Without meaning to, I say this like a command. I feel the power of my magic as soon as the words fly out of my mouth.

Claudine's eyes glass over for a few seconds. She blinks and shakes her head like she's clearing it. "Okay."

Instantly, guilt washes over me. I didn't intend to command Claudine using the gayuma's magic. But this is Claudine's party. She should be in the limelight. Besides, she seems comfortable holding the microphone. This is definitely not the first time she's used it. "If you don't want to—"

"It's okay." Claudine stands up. "But you choose the song."

I already went through the list while Tita Raven was testing the mic. "Song number seven-seven-twenty-one. 'Let It Go' by Idina Menzel."

As the opening notes start booming from the videoke machine's giant speakers, Angelou, Marvin, Bobby, Judy, and Ann take their seats at our table. Behind them, the clear windows show the sun falling to the horizon.

Claudine grins, and I grin back. I can't believe that this is the same girl who embarrassed me in front of everyone just last week.

Let it go.

Yep. That's the perfect song to end this perfect day.

For now.

CHAPTER SIXTEEN

The Sea of Cotton Candy

Claudine is currently in Cebu with her mother, but I'm glad to be able to have some time off from being around her. There are things I want to sort out about Claudine, particularly my conflicting feelings about being friends with her for real.

All week since her birthday party, Claudine and I have been sending chat messages nonstop. She tells me about her day with her tutor, while I tell her about public school.

Homeschooling sounds pretty cool—her homework sounds really challenging but interesting. Claudine says she loves hearing about my day in public school too. She sent a bunch of laughing emojis and GIFs after I told her how the twins and Marvin fell all over themselves when they tried to catch a live chicken in agriculture class. I did fairly well with that one. After all, I get a lot of practice at home chasing after Lolo Sebyo's chickens with Kidlat.

Saturday is potion lessons day with Lolo Sebyo. It's always been the highlight of my week. Today, I just don't feel like brewing anything. But I need to get my head back into brewing this Positive Thinking potion before my grandfather's lab blows up.

"You have to concentrate, my Bee," Lolo Sebyo says. Maybe I'm being paranoid, but I think I hear a hint of frustration in his voice. "Potion making requires focus. You do not want to excite the potion too much. Now you add the positivity essence, just one drop and—"

I pour a third of the bottle into the potion before Lolo can finish his instruction. The green liquid turns cotton-candy pink in an instant.

"Carefully, Bee!" He tries to save the potion, but it's too late. The essence has already bonded with the rest of the brew.

"Oh no!"

My failed, now-pink brew puffs up, doubling in size. It's taken on the texture of whipped cream, increasing in volume by the second. Lolo Sebyo turns off the heat, but the pink foam has already covered the entire table, me, and Lolo Sebyo.

I wipe potion off my face. Of all my brewing mishaps,

this is by far the messiest and the prettiest. Lolo Sebyo and I look like we swam in a sea of cotton candy. "So that's what an 'excited potion' looks like."

Lolo Sebyo heaves a long sigh, taking the rags from the cupboard. "Your mind is obviously elsewhere. We might as well call it a day. What is bothering you, child?"

"Nothing po."

My grandpa raises an eyebrow. I've always wanted to do that. But whenever I try, both my brows shoot up my forehead instead of just one.

"Okay, Lolo." I really can't tell Lolo Sebyo the *whole* truth. "I was thinking about going out for a swim. I haven't really explored the island yet. And I've been here, what? About half a year already?"

"Fair enough." He tosses me a rag. "Help me clean this up and you should be good to go."

"Thank you po."

"What's going on? What's all that pink stuff?"

Lolo Sebyo and I stop cleaning and look up. Claudine is standing in the doorway.

My eyes grow wide. No, she can't be here. I don't want Claudine to see where I live. It's embarrassing!

"Sorry. Your dad let me in." Claudine walks over to where Lolo Sebyo is and asks for his hand. "Mano po, Tatay Sebyo."

"Claudine Dimasalang! Peachy's beautiful daughter."

He blesses her with the sign of the cross in the air. "What brings you here?"

"There's something I wanted to show Jolina. I hope it's okay?"

I look expectantly at Lolo. This is what I've been hoping for all morning—a break from potion making. Besides, the sooner I get Claudine out of our house, the better.

Don't get me wrong. I'm proud of my family. But Claudine lives in this huge mansion. Our house looks like a shack by the sea compared to hers. I don't know what I'll do if she makes fun of it.

"Go ahead, Bee." Lolo Sebyo gives me a kind smile. "I will finish the cleanup. Don't make your friend wait."

"Thank you, Lolo."

Well, I'm not sure if Claudine is *really* my friend. Can you call a "friendship" based on gayuma real?

Anyway, friend or not, I'm glad to be out of potion class early. Claudine and I bid Lolo Sebyo farewell, with Kidlat following close behind. I have no idea what Claudine wants to show me. To my surprise, she leads me straight to the mango tree in our yard, where two bikes with baskets are parked against it.

Claudine pats the shiny blue one. "Mommy and I were in Cebu all week. I told her you had to sell your bike when you moved here so you couldn't ride with me. She got me another one so we can ride together!"

"Oh wow." I touch the handlebars of the red bike, the

very same bike I admired in Claudine's bedroom. It's so beautiful. "I can't take this."

If she hadn't been so pleased seeing me wear that blue-and-green floral blouse I ordered her to buy using gayuma, I would have returned it. I don't know. After seeing another side of her at the party, it just doesn't feel right having her buy things for me.

"Why not?" Claudine's lips curl into a pout. "I thought you liked it."

"I do. But this is too much." I shake my head. As much as I want to, it just feels so wrong. I don't like having someone giving me expensive things that I can't afford just to get me to hang out with them. It makes me feel . . . I don't know. Cheap. "I can't take this, Claudine."

"Fine," Claudine grumbles. She meets my gaze, her eyes expectant. "How about if I let you borrow it? I just really want to go biking with you. Bring Kidlat along too. That's what the basket is for."

Woof! Woof! Kidlat runs in a circle, barking excitedly.

Well, I guess borrowing works. "Okay. But on one condition."

"What?"

"You're going to let me bring the picnic food." I point at the basket attached to Claudine's blue bike.

Claudine grins. "Deal!"

I hurry to the eatery and grab a bunch of ready-to-eat snacks and a few bottles of mineral water. When I return,

Claudine is sitting on the bench outside Lolo's potion lab, whistling a tune that sounds a lot like "Let It Go."

"What did you get?" she asks, her face lighting up when she sees me.

"Chicken adobo pandesal," I answer. "If you want something else—"

"No! I love chicken adobo pandesal. It's perfect!" Claudine takes our picnic provisions and places them in her bike basket. She looks back at me. "So what's the pink foam stuff?"

I thought Claudine would forget all about what she saw in Lolo Sebyo's potion lab but apparently not.

"Nothing. Just some soap that got out of hand." It's such a pathetic excuse, but it's all I can think of.

"It didn't smell like soap. It was kind of like my body spray—like cotton candy." Claudine meets my gaze, frowning. "You know, if you don't want to tell me, just say so. You don't have to lie."

"It's supposed to be a Positive Thinking potion."

"Ah. I see." Claudine flicks pink foam off my hair. "Is it supposed to be so foamy?"

My eyes narrow. "No."

"Hey, chill!" Claudine holds up her hand in surrender. "I'm just trying to lighten the mood."

"Sorry." I let out a long sigh. "I'm just having so much trouble with brewing. Lolo says I'm doing well for someone who just started five months ago, but it doesn't feel like it. Everything I make just ends up being a huge, colossal failure."

Well, except for the gayuma, that is. But of course, I can't tell her that.

"You should trust your lolo. He's the best arbularyo there is. If he says you're doing good, you're doing good," Claudine says. "I heard Ate Rica and our driver, Kuya Tinio, talking about him before. Kuya Tinio said he drove Mommy and a group of resort customers from Manila to your house once. Mommy needed your lolo's help for her customers. These people explored an off-limits area at the resort and accidentally angered an engkanto with their noise. Tatay Sebyo cured them. He is *that* good."

"Yeah, he is," I agree.

"It's really cool that you'll be saving people one day."

"It *is* cool." I grin. "That is, if I ever get past making pink foam."

"The pink foam's cool. Useless but cool."

We laugh. It's nice to laugh with someone who is human and actually my age.

Claudine dusts her hands. "You ready to go?"

I secure Kidlat in the basket and get on Claudine's red bike. "Yep! Where to, Miss Navigator?"

"I know a place." Claudine wiggles her eyebrows. "But can you keep up, Manilenya?"

I'm surprised that for the first time ever, I'm not offended when she calls me Manilenya. Well, for one, she says it without malice. For another, I get this feeling she only means it in jest. Like, somehow, I now belong in her world—I'm no longer an outsider.

I give her a wink. "Bring it on, Claudine."

CHAPTER SEVENTEEN

The Lighthouse of Mount Mahal

Kidlat and I follow Claudine through Isla Pag-Ibig. We ride our bikes in the middle of the paved roads, moving to the side for the occasional vehicles passing by. They're fast, but so few that drivers have ample time to slow down for us. Every now and then, we see a group of teens hanging out at the roadside, their backs on the metal guard rails, playing with their phones.

Claudine is leading us to the north side of the island, where we pass by rice fields at the foot of Mount Mahal. Then the foliage begins to thicken. Shrubs and towering trees hide dirt paths leading to the forests, but Claudine keeps us on the road.

Soon the trees lessen, and we're greeted once again by a view of the beach. We pedal harder as the slope becomes steeper and finally reach the top, where a lighthouse stands.

"We're not allowed at the tower, so let's just set up there." Claudine points to a nipa hut a few meters from the lighthouse, under two coconut trees and in front of a giant rock. It has a bamboo table in the middle and benches of the same material on its opposite sides. "Tourists visit this a lot for selfies and photo shoots during the summer. That hut has the best view of the Philippine Sea in all of Isla Pag-Ibig. Even better than the view from our resort—but don't tell Mommy that."

I laugh. Claudine is surprisingly funny.

"So you like it?" She stares at me intently. Odd.

"Yeah. What's not to like?" I park the bike near the hut and help Kidlat out of the basket. He runs straight for the grassy area, sniffing around.

"My cousins from Manila visited last summer, before you moved here. They didn't like it here. They just took selfies and insisted we go back to the resort so they could swim. They find it boring, just watching the waves and all."

"Well, I'm not like them," I assure her. "Kidlat and I spend hours just staring at the beach behind Lolo's house. And the view isn't even this gorgeous. Can you help me with this? This ride got me really hungry."

Claudine's expression clears. She grins and helps me unload our picnic stuff from her basket and our back-packs. "You're always eating."

"I love food." I shrug. "And I live above a carinderia."

"Good point," Claudine says with a chuckle. She takes

the other end of the picnic blanket, and we bring it over the table, watching it float down and settle on the uneven bamboo wood.

I hand Claudine a couple of bread rolls with shredded chicken adobo.

Philippine adobo is unlike the adobo stuff they use in Mexican cuisine. "Adobo" just means cooking meat, seafood, or veggies marinated in soy sauce, vinegar, garlic, and black peppercorns. Dad's chicken adobo is the best—it's slightly sweet and has a hint of spice. I really love making flakes out of the chicken, stuffing them between two pandesal halves, and lathering the meat with the adobo sauce. It's the perfect afternoon snack. And because the vinegar helps it stay fresh longer, it's also the best picnic meal.

"Oh, this is so good!" Claudine exclaims as she downs her food with water. She takes another huge bite and swallows. "I can't get enough of it."

"Slow down!" I say, laughing. I take my own giant bite out of the pandesal. The adobo chicken and bread roll combination is sweet and spicy and salty and sour.

"I miss going to this lighthouse. Mom and Tita Raven used to bring me here all the time, but they're too busy to do that now. I feel safe around here, like it's that one thing I will always see if I get lost in the dark," Claudine says. She gives me a smile as she dusts bread crumbs off her shorts. "I'm glad you're here with me."

"Same," I say sincerely, smiling back. "Thanks for bringing me here."

Riding to the lighthouse with Kidlat and Claudine is so far the best experience I've had since moving here. We take a million selfies like tourists, making weird poses with Kidlat beside the giant rocks and on the beach. We don't go into the water though. There are a lot of tiny jellyfish hiding under the floating seaweed. No selfie is worth a painful jellyfish sting.

By the time we arrive at Nanay Dadang's sari-sari store, it's already half past three. Thankfully, a man selling balut—hard-boiled, fertilized duck eggs—passes by, so Claudine and I have something to eat again. I try to pay for the eggs I get for Kidlat and me, but Claudine insists on paying.

"You already made those delicious adobo rolls. It's my turn now," she says.

Well, I won't say no to free balut!

"Thanks," I say, cracking the pointy side of my boiled duck egg on the trunk of a palm tree. "Do you ever wonder why foreigners bet each other to eat balut?"

"Well, it does look weird, you know." Claudine removes a broken shell off her own balut. "I mean, look at that underdeveloped duck embryo. That thing looks like a real bird. I only eat the yolk part, but people who eat the bird say it's really good. But it's really gross-looking."

"Yeah, it is." I sip the soup from the egg. It's very gamey and flavorful. "I don't eat the bird either. Kidlat does that for me!"

At the mention of his name, my dog stands on his hind legs as he leans on me. Giggling, I pick the embryo from the egg and give it to him. Kidlat gobbles it whole, then runs around in circles happily.

"He really loves you," Claudine says, smiling at Kidlat.

"Of course! Kidlat is the best boy." I scratch Kidlat behind his ears. The dog closes his eyes in bliss.

"You're lucky he's very loyal to you." Claudine puts some rock salt on her balut. "I used to have a goldfish, but one day Winter ate it. Mommy said the fish did a Sagip on me."

"Sagip?"

"Seriously?" Claudine's eyes go wide. "You're an arbularyo apprentice of a famous faith healer and a descendant of Isla Pag-Ibig's oldest magical family, and you don't know what a Sagip is?"

"I *am* still in training, you know." I'm starting to like Claudine, but sometimes she can really be tactless. I don't need to be reminded that I'm this outsider who knows nothing about what's common and basic knowledge to people in Isla Pag-Ibig.

"A Sagip is when an animal sacrifices its life to save you from bad luck or an illness." Claudine sighs in frustration, like she's explaining Sagip to a stubborn little toddler. "So, anyway, I was so sad when Winter ate my fish, but Mommy said the fish must have done a Sagip on me—"

"That doesn't make any sense." I chew the yolk and swallow. "Cats eat fish. The fish couldn't have knowingly sacrificed itself for you."

"*Anyway . . .*" Claudine rolls her eyes. She does that often around me, making me wonder if I accidentally broke the gayuma spell or something. "That fish loved me. I was so sad when Winter ate it."

"Okay." I toss the empty balut shell in the bushes. Lolo Sebyo says duck eggs make good fertilizers. "But did you get saved?"

"I dunno." Claudine eats the last of her balut's yolk and gives the embryo to Kidlat. My dog laps it up happily. "I still got a cold the next day. Maybe it could have been worse?"

I tilt my head, pretending to be deep in thought. "Maybe the fish just didn't like you as much as you thought it did."

"Ha, ha." Claudine sticks her yolk-covered tongue at me. Gross. "You're *so* hilarious."

We look at each other and burst out laughing.

"What's so funny?" a voice calls from across the road.

Angelou and Marvin are walking toward us, eating ice candy.

"Hey-o," Angelou greets us. She waves her papaya ice candy. Kidlat is eyeing it with interest. "We're going to play billiards at Tatay Goryo's. Want to join us?"

"That sounds fun!" I can't believe it took me so long to start talking to these two. Angelou and Marvin are very nice. I hang out with them and the twins during recess at school now.

Claudine only sees them in Bible study though, so I'm not surprised she's hesitant to join them. Angelou and Marvin went to Claudine's party, but seeing them in school every day is not the same as seeing someone just once a week. Especially when you're like Claudine, who doesn't make friends easily.

"I can just watch you play, if you really want to go." Claudine bites her lower lip. "Do you know how to play?"

Hmm. Last week, Claudine would have agreed to go with me without question. Maybe the gayuma really is starting to wear off.

"Well, there was a billiard place near our apartment in Marikina. I'm not the best, but I know the basics. I can teach you, if you want." With a little push, I might be able to invoke the gayuma magic and make Claudine agree. I miss playing billiards. But I don't know. I don't want to push it. If Claudine really doesn't want to play, then that's fine with me. I had so much fun today because of her. It doesn't feel right to force her into something she obviously feels iffy about.

"Promise you'll teach me?" Claudine looks me straight in the eye. "Promise you won't laugh if I'm awful?"

"I promise."

"Angelou and I don't know how to play either," Marvin says with a chuckle. "Jolina will have to teach us all."

"I can do that." I grin. This game is sounding more fun by the minute.

"Okay. I'm in," Claudine says.

Angelou, Marvin, and I cheer. Kidlat joins in with his barking. I doubt he knows what we're happy about. He just knows we're happy, so he's happy too.

"We don't have bikes, so we better start walking," Marvin says. "See you at Tatay Goryo's?"

"See you!" I say.

I strap Kidlat inside the bike basket and ask Claudine, "Do you know where Tatay Goryo's is? I should have asked Marvin. But I assumed you'd know—"

"Yeah, I do. I know where it is." Claudine puts a hand on my arm and looks down. "I just gotta ask . . . Do you wish you were back home in Metro Manila? We don't have billiards places everywhere, or those fancy Italian restaurants."

I smile. "No. I'm already home."

If she'd asked me this question a month ago, Claudine would have gotten another answer. But things change. I'm probably still the same, but there are things I see differently now. And when I really think about it, I have to admit it's got a lot to do with her.

Claudine returns my smile and gets on her bike. I watch

her wave at Angelou and Marvin, who are now starting their trek to Tatay Goryo's.

It was so easy, when I decided to give Claudine the gayuma. But now I think it was a rather rash decision. There were so many things I didn't know about Claudine. Like her insecurities. Her so-called friends. Her kindness beneath that irritating bluntness.

I'm really starting to enjoy being her friend.

The book says that the magic can either make things better or worse between us. I won't know for sure until the gayuma wears off. If all goes well, she'll still be my friend because of the time she spent getting to know me. But if not, she might hate me forever.

CHAPTER EIGHTEEN

A Starry Night of Sorries and Whatnots

We arrive home just in time for sundown. Claudine doesn't like biking or walking in the dark, so she'll have to call home and arrange to have their family driver pick her up. But Mom invites her for dinner, and Claudine happily accepts.

"I called Mommy and she says I can stay!" Claudine bounces into the kitchen, where I'm helping Dad prepare mango ensalada. "Anything I can do to help?"

"How would you like to be on grill duty with me, young lady?" Lolo Sebyo takes a tray of stuffed bangus wrapped in foil from the counter. "You can even bring home to your mother some of the fish and liempo you'll grill yourself."

"Yes, sir! I would love to. Mommy is going to be so happy." Claudine takes the other tray, which is full of marinated lechon belly, and follows Lolo Sebyo to the backyard.

Kidlat walks to the door as it closes behind Claudine. He loves it whenever we grill pork belly in the yard. He always gets pieces of meat whenever Lolo Sebyo is the one in charge of the grill. He stares at the door, then looks back at me.

"It's okay, good boy. You can go with them if you want."

Kidlat whines. He takes one longing look at the door but ultimately walks to where I'm standing and lies near my feet.

"Aww, that's so sweet," Mom remarks as she enters the kitchen from the eatery. "I've closed up. Time for rest!"

Mom turns on the television and tunes into the news.

Dad rinses my peeler and hands me a knife and a tomato, then begins chopping the onions and the unripe mangoes. He always takes the harder tasks whenever we're cooking together. Not because he doesn't think I can do it, but because he just wants to make things easier for me.

"Dad, how come you never became an arbularyo? You love to cook, and cooking isn't so different from potion making." He also has the selflessness required of arbular-yos, which, admittedly, I sometimes struggle with.

"That's true. But like Papa said, magic skips generations. It definitely skipped me." Dad stops chopping and looks at me. "Come to think of it, I'm glad I can't do magic. It's such a huge responsibility. I'm really proud of you, Bee."

There's a loud chime from the TV. The weather lady then comes on. "There is a low-pressure system building up in the Pacific. We will know in the next few days if it develops into a tropical depression. In the meantime, we urge everyone to stay dry—"

Mom sighs and turns the TV off. She joins Dad and me in the kitchen. "I hope the rain eases up. It's been getting harder and harder to get to work with these rains."

I get what she means. Sometimes we get blessed with a sunny, fun afternoon just like the one Claudine and I had. The only thing predictable during the wet season in the Philippines is the fact that it will rain, one way or another. We were lucky it didn't start pouring out of the blue.

Mom takes a dirty plate and starts clearing the counter.

"I'll clean that later, hon," Dad says, gently taking the plate from her. "Get some rest."

"Thanks, love." Mom leans her head on Dad's shoulder. "You take such good care of me."

"Of course. Anything for you." Dad gives Mom a quick kiss on the lips.

"Eww!" I groan.

Mom and Dad laugh. They kiss me sloppily on either cheek.

Kidlat tries to join in, jumping on his hind legs until one of us also gives him a kiss on the forehead.

This is what love is all about. And friendship. Mom tells

me that friendship is also a kind of love. Since the love between Mom and Dad is different than friendship, of course.

This is the kind of genuine relationship Claudine deserves, I realize with a pang. Not the friendship I dragged her into—a friendship born out of anger and revenge.

After dinner, while waiting for Claudine's driver to pick her up, Kidlat and I bring Claudine to the beach behind Lolo Sebyo's backyard.

"The sand's muddy looking and full of pebbles, unlike the beaches at your resort and behind your house and the lighthouse, but the sky is nice from here." I'm sure Claudine has seen even prettier beaches since she and her mom travel a lot in the Visayas and Mindanao regions. But it's all we have and what I can offer her.

"I love it," Claudine says. She sits on a fallen coconut tree, with her legs crossed beneath her. "The night sky is so close, I feel like I can touch the stars."

Kidlat and I join her on the log. I smile. "Kidlat and I always come here whenever the sky's as clear as this."

Claudine points to the sky. "Those three stars are Orion's Belt. And the whole thing is Orion. That bright one is the North Star."

I try to find the stuff she's talking about. "They all look the same to me."

"You have to use your imagination a bit." She traces her finger to the sky. "See? Orion looks like a man. His belt is where his waist is."

I really can't see it. "Well, they are very pretty."

"You're hopeless." Claudine laughs.

I laugh along with her. We seem to be laughing a lot when we're together. "Yeah. I guess am."

A silence falls between us. But it's a comfortable silence. We listen to the waves rushing to the shore, the wind rustling tree leaves, and the occasional snore of Kidlat sleeping soundly between us.

Claudine is the first to break the silence. "You know something I realized?"

"What?"

"I had a friend named Antonette, or I thought I did. I don't think she was really my friend." She looks up at the stars, a thoughtful expression on her face. "We were always together when she still lived here. But I don't think I really mattered to her. She was only 'friends' with me because our parents have business together and we attended the same Bible study group. Other than that, we didn't have anything in common. She fits in well with Maui and Selena, but I don't think I ever did. I'm the 'ugly one' in their group. I'm brown and not pretty enough. And my mommy . . . Mommy wasn't rich before. The girls were rich before their own parents were born."

I remember the way Selena talked about Claudine. I

didn't know Claudine back then as well as I do now, but I already knew her "friends" don't treat her fairly.

"They're wrong about you," I say more firmly than I intend. Those snobs just make me so angry. "Your being brown doesn't make you ugly. Mom always says we're beautiful. We just have this hang-up about white being pretty because it's what our Spanish and American colonizers wanted us to think."

Claudine runs a hand through her hair. "Thanks. That means a lot. Um . . . I'm not good with people and sometimes I say things without thinking about them first—"

"You don't say."

"Okay, okay. I *often* say things without thinking," Claudine says with a short laugh, but she quickly mellows down. "We got off on the wrong foot because of that, but . . ."

"Yes?"

"I was jealous of you." Claudine stares at her hands. "Your life in Metro Manila seemed so exciting, just like my cousins say it is. I couldn't blame you for being bored here . . . I just didn't want to think that I'm a boring probinsyana to you."

All along I'd been thinking she just hated me for no reason at all. That she looked down on me.

"You're far from being a boring provincial girl, Claudine." I shake my head. This was the last thing I thought she'd say. "And honestly, I think we're better off here. It's more peaceful and so beautiful with all these trees and the beaches and the nice people I've met." I smile at Claudine so she'll know I'm referring to her too. But I also want to make one thing clear. "You shouldn't be jealous of me. You're lucky your mom can buy anything you want. Not many people are born with that. Dad says that if we keep wanting things other people have, we won't get to enjoy the stuff we do have."

"Your dad is so smart—he's right and I know that now, thanks to you. I'm used to having friends who take this stuff for granted . . ." Claudine lets out a long sigh. "I'm used to taking everything for granted. Then I met your family, and I see things differently now, and I feel so bad about everything and . . . What I'm trying to say is . . . I'm sorry for being so insensitive. I promise I'll try to do better and, um . . . I'm really very sorry for embarrassing you in Bible study. I thought you were mocking me, and I just got so angry that I didn't think straight. That last invite wasn't for Mr. Bradbury—it was always for you."

I'm such a terrible person. I'm so awful, giving gayuma to a girl who sincerely wanted to be friends with me.

"I felt so bad about it," Claudine continues, picking up a fistful of the dark sand. "I figured maybe I could invite you through your mom. Tita Sunshine talks about you a lot whenever I'm at the resort. She often says you're the best kid any mom could ask for, so I knew you couldn't say no if she asked you to attend my party. Then I'd let you meet Winter, and maybe you'd see I'm not really bad since a cat likes me. But for some reason, I couldn't stop thinking about you. I felt like I needed to do something really drastic. So I made this special invite. Like, go big on it, you know?"

All I can do is nod.

"What I'm trying to say is . . ." Claudine lets the sand fall between her fingers. "I'm really, really sorry."

A lump forms in my throat. Why, oh why, did I ever use gayuma on this good person?

"You don't have to forgive me." Claudine wipes a tear with the back of her clean hand. "I just want to let you know how sorry I am."

I think about the past few months and how angry I was at Claudine. I think about the times I thought she was insulting me, but she just didn't know how to say the words correctly.

Like Lolo Sebyo said, there are people who have forgotten how to express their kindness even though they've always been kind deep inside. Claudine is definitely this person.

Had I known this, would I have given her the kindness potion instead of the gayuma? I might have. And I wouldn't be in this position, where I have no idea if the friendship she feels for me is real.

But I do know that what I feel about her is real. She is *my* friend.

I loop my arm around hers. "Thank you for being my friend."

"Thanks too." Claudine squeezes my arm. "I'm so glad I have you and Kidlat now."

I also owe Claudine an apology. I judged her too harshly. Though I can't bring myself to say sorry. Not because I don't want to, but because I feel it won't be 100 percent sincere. To be truly sincere, I will have to admit and apologize for a more terrible thing—that I used gayuma on her.

I wish we could stay like this forever. But whatever I've done wrong so far, I'll be a worse person if I let this continue. I have to lift the spell . . . even if it means never seeing Claudine again.

CHAPTER NINETEEN

Bittersweet Farewell Candies

It's already past nine when Claudine leaves. I wait until Lolo Sebyo has retreated to his room and my parents have said good night to me before I sneak out to the potion lab.

"Let's go get this gayuma spell lifted, Kidlat," I whisper to my dog. He jumps excitedly but doesn't bark. Kidlat knows we need to be quiet, or the adults will hear. He doesn't approve of what I've done (and I don't blame him), but my dog wouldn't do anything to get me in trouble. He's such a smart, good dog.

I turn the lights on in the lab. Making a brew in the dark would be catastrophic, and I've already made such a mess of things as it is. Some herbs look very similar, and I need to be sure I'm putting the right ones in.

The gayuma reversion spell is surprisingly easy. For one,

there are so many sources about it in Lolo Sebyo's library. For another, I don't need to give Claudine anything. A very experienced arbularyo like Lolo Sebyo wouldn't even need to make a potion. He'd just utter chants and prayers over a lighted candle under the moon, and it would all be over. But I'm obviously not like Lolo—far from it—so I have to do it the hard way.

Kidlat's lying right beside me with a paw on my foot. He's worried about me.

"This will be over soon, little guy," I promise him. "Can you move there a little just in case something goes wrong? I don't want to spill anything on you."

But Kidlat won't budge.

"All right. Just be on your guard, okay?"

I light the pink candle I used before and begin putting the stuff in the palayok.

A sage leaf
Three whole leaves from a
calamansi tree
Grated root of ginger
A pinch of ground tawas crystal
A printed photograph of the person
who received the gayuma

I put everything in, then say the reversion chant. "Oh!"

A tiny flame forms at the bottom of Claudine's photo. I try to put it out, but it won't let me. I touch the flames, and they don't feel hot at all. They simply eat up Claudine's photo until it's nothing but a pile of ash on the table.

Woof! Kidlat lets out a soft bark and whines like he's scared. He covers his eyes with his paws.

"It's okay now, good boy. No more fire. You can look." I take the ash and sprinkle it in the potion, but nothing happens.

I stir the potion as instructed. Still, nothing happens. I wait for a few seconds before stirring again, but the potion just stays the same—a potful of stuff but without the magic.

The fire under the palayok is still going strong as it should be, and yet my potion isn't even boiling. It's just . . . there.

My gayuma reversion didn't work, I realize with a sinking feeling in my stomach. I can't get Claudine out of this spell.

There's only one person who can.

CHAPTER TWENTY

The Magic of Forgiveness

Lucky for me, Lolo Sebyo is still awake.

He listens intently as I tell him what happened. Every single detail, starting from that day on the river when Claudine poked fun at me for swimming with a bathing carabao. I tell him about wanting to get Mom promoted. I tell him about the love and friendship I didn't expect to feel with Claudine. I tell him everything.

"Oh, my Bee." Lolo Sebyo peers into the palayok with my failure of a potion. "I'm disappointed in you. What do I always tell you about using magic? About our intentions?"

His words cut my heart more intensely than it would have had he shouted at me instead.

"To use it only for good and for helping people." I hang my head in shame. "I'm so sorry, Lolo. I was just so angry!"

"I know, my child," he says, stirring the failed potion with a stick. "I should have followed my instincts when you asked about the kindness potion. And I should have been more up front with you about gayuma."

Okay, now I feel even worse. Lolo Sebyo is blaming himself for my very selfish mistake. "No, Lolo. This is on me."

"Unfortunately, the magic agrees with you." My grandfather lets out a long sigh. "Do you remember the first lesson I ever gave you when I decided to take you on as my apprentice?"

"Yes, Lolo." I nod. "It was about Balik. You get what you give."

I remember it clearly. We were sitting on the bench by his potion lab when I got initiated as the "official" Bagayan arbularyo-in-traing. Lolo guided me through the most basic of magical concepts: Balik. Whatever you give, you'll also receive. Do good, you get rewarded with good fortune. Do bad, you get punished with bad.

"That is correct," says Lolo, leaning over the clay pot to sniff my potion. "But like I have told you before, the gayuma is a dangerous potion to brew. Arbularyos avoid making it if they can—unless they have long abandoned their morality and no longer care about consequence. That is why you don't see many books written about it. You see, the gayuma is the only potion that always has a negative Balik."

"What do you mean, Lolo?" I have a bad feeling I know the answer, and it's not good.

My grandfather stops sniffing the pot and looks up to meet my gaze. "Using something as pure as love to control another—there is simply nothing good in that."

"Oh no." The butterflies in my stomach turn to frenzy. I lean on the table, willing myself not to throw up.

Woof. Something wet touches my knee. I look down and find Kidlat staring at me. I calm down a bit. That is, until—

"I agree," Lolo says, nodding. "'Oh no' indeed."

Irritation overshadows my worry. I narrow my eyes. Okay, I deserve the punishment. But my *grandfather* can at least be afraid for me, even just a teeny bit. Kidlat moves closer to me. His body heat calms me once more.

"I'm sorry, my Bee. I do not mean to offend you." He ruffles my hair. "I'm not worried because I'm certain you will deflect the Balik."

That's reassuring but not reassuring enough. "But how po, Lolo?"

"The Balik begins seven days after you lift the spell." Lolo Sebyo stirs the potion and sniffs it again. I wish he'd tell me why he keeps smelling and stirring it. "Reversing the gayuma didn't work not because you didn't do it right, but because the spell has been lifted already. True love—true friendship—broke the magic's hold on the Dimasalang girl."

I remember earlier tonight at the beach, when Kidlat, Claudine, and I were under the stars. Claudine said she was glad we're friends. I tell Lolo all about it.

"Do you believe that is when both of you acknowledged that your friendship is real?" Lolo Sebyo asks.

I nod. Claudine and I were just biking and eating most of the day. We didn't really have a serious talk until this evening, before she left.

"I see. Then starting at that moment, magic has given you seven days to right your wrong. After which your Balik will come." Lolo Sebyo smiles sadly. "I told you, gayuma magic is a complicated one."

I rub the back of my neck. "But how do I make things right? I made a huge mess of things, Lolo."

"Do not lose hope," my grandpa says as he throws the contents of the palayok into the sink. "All you need to do is ask for and receive forgiveness from your friend."

Kidlat gives my foot a nudge, like he's telling me that he agrees with Lolo.

"I can ask, but I doubt she'll forgive me." If someone did the same thing to me, I'm not sure I'd be able to forgive them. I'm having trouble even forgiving myself.

"She will." Lolo Sebyo gives me a reassuring smile. "Like with the kindness potion, the gayuma would not have worked as well as it did had Claudine not felt any fondness for you. She must have wanted to become your friend already even before you gave her the gayuma. That is a true love that will forgive you and save you from Balik."

Hearing this should make me feel better, but it doesn't. It makes me feel worse. Claudine has been a true friend to me all along, and she deserves to know the truth.

I need to be the true friend to Claudine that she is to me.

CHAPTER TWENTY-ONE
Typhoon Totoy

Unfortunately, the worsening weather doesn't make it easy for me. School gets canceled the very next day, and the torrential rains make it impossible for me to meet with Claudine at Nanay Dadang's. It's not just bad weather—it's a typhoon.

The government agency in charge of tracking the typhoon is the PAGASA, or the Philippine Atmospheric, Geophysical and Astronomical Services Administration. They even named the tropical cyclone "Typhoon Totoy," an innocent-sounding name for a dangerous storm. Typhoon Totoy is expected to bring strong winds and storm surges to Isla Pag-Ibig, so everyone in town is rushing to prepare for it.

Schools, resorts, and business establishments have all closed down—the Bagayan Food Haus is one of them. Everything is closed and canceled because of the storm. Even mass and Bible study have been canceled.

I asked Lolo Sebyo if getting forgiven via video call counts, but he couldn't be sure. We both agreed that it's best to do it in person though. A call or a text just wouldn't come across right, and I can't afford to get the tone wrong. Mom might lose her promotion—or worse, her job—if Claudine gets mad at me.

Besides, I've already tried to text Claudine to ask how she is, but I couldn't get a cell phone signal. The typhoon is steadily becoming more dangerous, damaging a lot of structures and facilities on the island.

On Thursday, PAGASA insists we head for our assigned evacuation centers, because Typhoon Totoy is set to arrive and Barangay San Pedro is no longer safe. By Friday, military trucks arrive to pick us up.

One of our neighbors refuses to evacuate. He doesn't want to leave his goats and pigs behind. He lives alone and the animals are the only family he has. I totally understand—I can't bear the thought of us leaving Kidlat and my grandfather's chickens behind. But unlike my dog and Lolo Sebyo's birds, there's just no room for his large pets in the trucks already crowded with people and their belongings.

The soldiers cuff and physically carry him into a caravan. He's assured by people from the provincial veterinary office that they will bring his pets to the evacuation center. Sure enough, the officers load his pigs and goats into an empty vehicle just as we leave the village.

I hug Kidlat tighter, burying my face into his fur. My ears pop as the truck climbs higher up the mountain terrain.

Two years ago, when we still lived in Marikina, we were forced to evacuate as Tropical Storm Karding flooded the city. But we had a car back then—we were able to bring as much stuff as our old sedan could carry. Now that we've sold the car and have to rely on the government's help, we have no choice but to leave most of our stuff behind.

I'm getting used to our life here in Isla Pag-Ibig. But I have to admit that I do miss the comforts of our old life in Metro Manila. Things were much easier when our family had a bit more money than we do now.

Before long, we finally arrive at the evacuation center.

The mayor's office has assigned people from our village to stay inside the Santa Elena Multipurpose Center, which they turned into a temporary shelter for us. Families from the other coastal town are staying at the Santa Elena Public School. Barangay Santa Elena is a village on the highest peak of Isla Pag-Ibig, near the cell phone tower. We should be safe here.

The people running the evacuation center put up square tents without ceilings inside the center—one for each family. The tents are arranged in neat columns with a narrow space between them so people can pass through.

Aw-ah-woo-hoo! Kidlat whines, biting at his leash as we walk through the center.

"I'm sorry, Kidlat." I lean down to pat my dog on the head. "The lady said you need to wear a leash every time you're outside our assigned tent or you can't stay with me. They'll put you in the shelter across the street with Lolo's chickens and other animals you don't know. Do you want that?"

Kidlat whines again, but he stops struggling. I breathe a sigh of relief. Mom had to beg the people at the door not to separate Kidlat from me. They weren't happy about it, but they eventually relented and allowed me to keep my dog.

"Jesus, Mary, and Joseph!" Dad huffs, dragging with him four large, packed-to-the-brim suitcases. He also carries two big duffel bags. "Did you pack the entire house, Papa?"

"Sus! Do not complain." Lolo Sebyo pokes one of the bags with his cane. "Those are priceless books, potions, and ingredients. It would be impossible to find replacements."

"Couldn't we leave them at the house and just put some magical protection on them or something?" Mom is panting as heavily as Dad. She's pulling a cart full of heavy boxes and more stuffed gym bags. "I feel like I've done twenty thousand reps of lifting weights pushing this thing. Honey, which one's our—"

"Excuse me po." A volunteer comes up to us, pushing a wheelchair. She tells Lolo Sebyo to use it so he won't have a hard time walking. "Tatay, gamitin nyo po itong wheelchair para di kayo mahirapan maglakad."

"Maraming salamat!" Lolo Sebyo thanks the woman.

I adjust the straps of my backpack as I watch Dad and the volunteer help my grandfather settle on the wheelchair. I wonder how far our assigned tent is for the volunteer to think Lolo Sebyo needs one.

"Sunod po kayo sa akin," a volunteer says, asking us to follow her. She guides us through the maze of numbered but identical blue tents in the evacuation center. I don't see any of the kids from school or Bible study. I hope I will so evacuation will be less lonely. But Lolo Sebyo is very popular. Everyone we pass by seems to know him.

I hold Kidlat's leash tighter. We could totally get lost in here if I don't pay attention to where we're going. I remind myself that the entrance doors are on the north side while the toilets are on the other end.

"These tents are great." Mom lets out a whistle. "I didn't think our little island would have the budget for this."

"Aren't they?" The volunteer beams. "They're mostly funded from donations from the private sector, but the mayor made certain the budget committee purchased these before the rainy season so we'd be prepared. And we are. We're probably the most prepared island in all of Bicol."

I wouldn't be surprised if Claudine's family was one of those that donated. Tita Peachy and Tita Raven do seem like the type of rich people who share their blessings.

The volunteer leads us farther into the shelter. About half the tents aren't occupied yet. But we did arrive early, being so close to the sea. The volunteer said more people are expected to come in within the day, and that we will be sharing the evacuation center with the people from Claudine's village. "A lot of them have already left the island though. Not surprising since their area covers the rich communities and the businesses by the port."

A trickle of excitement travels down my spine, sending goose bumps on my skin.

While the altruistic part of me hopes Claudine and her family are out of harm's way, the more selfish part of me hopes to see her here. As much as I feel terrible for what I did, I'd be lying if I said I didn't want to be forgiven. Because I do. I not only want to avoid Balik, but it would be great to keep being friends with Claudine too. I could use my friend during this scary time.

We've reached the toilets at the far end of the evacuation center when the volunteer finally stops.

"This is you," she says, pointing to tent number 283. "It's fortunate a tent in the corner near the windows and bleachers is empty so you get to keep your dog. Please make sure to keep him secured at all times. If anyone complains about him, we'll have no choice but to put him in the shelter."

The volunteer helps Lolo Sebyo get off the wheelchair. "I'm afraid I'll have to take this. There might be more evacuees needing it. But I'll be back with a chair for Tatay."

"Thank you," Mom says, but as soon as the volunteer

is out of earshot, she shakes a finger at Kidlat. "Hear that, fur-ball? You better behave or it's the shelter for you!"

Kidlat covers his face with his paws. We all laugh, including Lolo Sebyo.

"Sunshine and I will set up the banig inside and somehow make all this luggage fit. We are going to be the only family in this evacuation center with a library," Dad says in a commanding voice, the one he used to use when he ran the kitchen of the restaurant in Marikina. "Bee, help Lolo find a seat in the bleachers while we wait for the volunteer to return. Kidlat, you guard Bee and Lolo." Dad claps his hands together. "Got it? Okay. Everyone, on to your tasks. We got this!"

"Yes, sir!" Mom says with a mock salute.

Dad rolls his eyes.

I giggle and do as I'm told. "Let's sit on that bench, Lolo. That way, you don't need to climb the bleachers."

"I am fine." Lolo Sebyo grunts. "Bring a bunch of those books for me, Bee. I will just catch up on my reading."

"Okay po, Lolo."

Lolo Sebyo and I pick a bench beside Nanay Dadang and Nanay Concha playing cards and drinking beer. They have a cooler between them.

"Ah! Well, if it isn't my favorite Bagayans!" a familiar voice says.

"Magandang umaga po, Nanay Dadang, Nanay Concha,"

I greet the older women with a good morning as I balance a bunch of books in my left hand and keep Kidlat's leash secured in the other.

I wonder if the sisters have ice candy stowed in their cooler. "By any chance, did you bring any ice candies with you?"

Nanay Dadang bursts out in boisterous laughter. "I wish!"

Lolo Sebyo takes a seat on the bench.

"Join us in tong-its, Sebyo?" Nanay Dadang shuffles the cards. "There is more beer in the cooler. Your granddaughter can get one for you."

"No, thank you." Lolo Sebyo shows them his book. "I brought reading material."

"Of course he did." Dad appears, bringing Lolo Sebyo a water bottle. "He brought his entire library. He *made us* bring his entire library."

Dad gives me a wink before leaving, making me giggle. I sit beside Lolo Sebyo with my legs crossed under me. Kidlat jumps on the bench and crawls into my lap.

Nanay Dadang seems to still insist on talking to Lolo even though Lolo is obviously starting to read his book. "I would have brought my entire sari-sari store if I could. I heard the Ciervos chartered boats for their things days ago, before they got on that helicopter."

"Ah. The things money can buy," Nanay Concha says, taking a swig of her beer. "Can't carry money to the grave, but it can help you out of the grave in times like this."

I don't like eavesdropping on other people's conversations, but it's really hard to avoid when they're so close to you.

Nanay Dadang takes a card from the pile. "Not everyone wealthy left the island. Peachy Dimasalang refused to leave. My nephew is friends with their driver, Tinio. Peachy sent Tinio to assist her partner to the mainland with their things, but Peachy still insisted on staying until the last minute. So of course, Peachy's partner came back for her. It is too late to fly them and the girl out now."

Wait. What?

"I suppose it's understandable. Peachy worked hard to get where she is—"

"I'm sorry po." I can't help myself. I dread the answer but I need to know. "Ano po ibig nyo sabihin by 'the girl'?"

"Ah! Did you not know? Claudine stayed behind with her parents," Nanay Dadang says, turning around to face me. "Threw a nasty fit and locked herself and the cat in her bedroom. Peachy was afraid she'd jump off the helicopter if they forced her to leave."

"Raven still should have forced the girl to go with her." Nanay Concha shakes her head in disapproval.

Nanay Dadang shrugs and takes a sip of beer straight from the bottle. "That girl won't leave her mother. Great kid. Very loyal. Strong willed too."

I feel a surge of hope. Maybe I will get a chance to make everything right with Claudine.

Kidlat licks my hand. I look down at the dog in my lap, and he stares back at me with his soulful brown eyes. They look scared.

I stroke Kidlat's head. "It's okay, good boy. We're safe here—"

The strong wind's loud howl interrupts me, followed by the sound of glass shattering. Then, just when it seems like things can't get any worse, the electricity goes out, blanketing the center in total darkness.

CHAPTER TWENTY-TWO
The Ugly Truth

"Ow!" I accidentally poke myself in the eye trying to slap a mosquito away from my face.

Kidlat looks at me with his tongue out.

"Ha, ha, very funny." I know panting is a dog's way of sweating. But when you lack sleep and have to reapply anti-mosquito lotion for the twenty-millionth time, the littlest thing gets to you.

Being stuck in one place with people you don't know and nowhere to go is no fun. But our family's making the most of our time. Mom and Dad are helping out the people cooking food for evacuees. Lolo Sebyo does his part too— he provides free massages and healing oils for anyone who needs them.

I had a difficult time sleeping last night. I miss the comfort of my bed and the ease of doing things with electricity. Because we still don't have electricity since last night's blackout. PAGASA said they expect Typhoon Totoy will make landfall in Isla Pag-Ibig anytime today, so the electric company still needs to be shut down for safety reasons.

Kidlat lowers his ears. My heart melts.

"Aww. Come here, you," I say, pulling him close to me on the floor. Between the loud howling of winds, the pesky mosquitos, and the fear of having to ask Claudine for forgiveness, the only thing that helps me sleep at night on the hard concrete floor of the evacuation center is having Kidlat next to me. He snuggles under my blankets, comforting me. My dog truly is a blessing.

"Help me with this, Jolina?" Mom comes into our tent with a huge sack of corn still in their husks. "We're making ginataang mais for evacuees. A lot of them haven't had breakfast yet."

"Of course!" I help Mom set up a space in our tent to shuck corn. Dad's ginataang mais, a sweet rice porridge with corn kernels and coconut milk, is the best. I'm sure our neighbors in the evacuation center will enjoy this comfort food.

Kidlat buries himself under the pile of discarded corn silk and husk, making a small nest in which to take a nap. I envy the life of dogs sometimes. They live in the now, with no worries to bring them down. But they also love so purely that I doubt they'd ever get themselves in a bind where they needed to ask for forgiveness to avoid having their lives come crashing down. Unlike yours truly.

"Mom, why did you let me hang out with Claudine on a

school night that day? You know, when she asked you for my number?"

Mom stops mid-shuck. "Well, you were so sad about moving. I wanted you to have a friend here, honey Bee. And I was right—you and Claudine did become friends."

It seems that everyone but me knew that Claudine and I could be great friends. Maybe even Kidlat knew— that's why he still accepted Claudine even though she was mean to me.

Can't blame Mom for thinking that way though. Even in Manila, I didn't have anyone I could call my best friend besides my dog. The apartment we used to live in only had old people living in the complex. In school, everyone was friendly, but there wasn't anyone I could totally connect with. Not one of them knew my family can do magic.

I'm glad to know Mom wasn't bullied into allowing me to go out on a school night. But there's still one thing that bothers me. "Weren't you worried about losing your job if Claudine stopped being friends with me?"

"Oh, Jolina. My thoughtful, sweet honey Bee." Mom puts down the corn she's shucking and leans over to kiss me on the forehead. "Claudine's parents are good people— they wouldn't fire an employee just because the employee's daughter is no longer friends with their kid. Don't ever let my job influence the choices you make about your friends."

"Thanks, Mom."

That makes me feel better. Claudine might never forgive

me and I'll suffer the consequences of Balik. But at least Mom will still have her job.

Maybe magic is giving me a chance to fix things, or it's just some weird coincidence. Through the unzipped door of our tent, I glimpse a familiar outline enter the nearby toilet—I'm pretty sure it's Claudine.

I jump to my feet, spilling bits of corn all over Kidlat. My dog happily eats them up. "I need to go to the toilet, Mom."

Before Mom can answer, I make my way out of the tent, now certain of what I need to do.

I wrinkle my nose while standing by the bathrooms.

Finally, Claudine steps out of the toilet.

"Hi," I say.

"Oh, hey! I wanted to text you but I couldn't get a signal. This typhoon is really bad. When did you get here? I'm so glad you're here now," she says, her face lighting up. "I'd give you a hug, but you know . . ."

"Nah, I'm good." I wrinkle my nose. "Didn't you wash your hands?"

"I did, but have you seen the sink inside? I could wash my hands until I scrubbed off my skin, but I'd still be dirty. So gross."

I laugh. I missed hearing Claudine's wisecracks in person. Fessing up is going to be harder than I thought.

"Where's Kidlat?"

"He's with Mom and Dad. They're helping make food for everyone," I say with pride. I might be a terrible person for using gayuma, but I do have the best parents. "They say Kidlat's presence helps people calm down."

"Cool. I'm sure he does. He calms *me* down. Good thing they let him stay with you," says Claudine, nodding. "They wanted to bring Winter to the animal shelter, but I just couldn't let them. Good thing Mommy convinced the barangay watchmen to let her stay with me."

"My mom talked to them too." I shift my feet. Like me, my feet are eager to leave this uncomfortable and smelly spot and go back to our tent and hide. Because for once, I have no idea what to say. I mean, really. What do you tell a person you befriended by giving them gayuma? Since she's blocking my way and I have nowhere to go, I say the first thing on my mind. "Where are you staying?"

"At the corner near the door." Claudine points at the north entrance. "How long have you been here?"

"Since yesterday. We're there." I point to the opposite side from where she's pointing. "It stinks but it's near a window and I get to keep Kidlat."

"Wanna hang at our tent? Mom let me bring some of my board games. We have chocolate, candy, potato chips—"

"Claudine, there's something I need to tell you." I rub the back of my neck. My insides feel like they're quivering. It's now or never. Either Claudine will forgive me and prevent my Balik, or hate me forever and doom me with bad luck.

"Can't it wait? There's so much I gotta tell you!" Claudine loops her arm around mine and continues to chat away. "Mom wanted me to go with Tita Raven to the mainland to stay with Tita Raven's parents, but I didn't want to, so—"

"Claudine! I'm serious." I pull my arm away and put my hands on her shoulders. "This is important."

"What?"

I stare at her face. My friend's beautiful face—her deep-set eyes and slightly pointy nose. I drink it all in. Because if this confession doesn't work out the way I hope it will, this might be the last time I see her without contempt in her eyes.

"None of this is real," I say softly, my voice barely above a whisper. "We're friends now but our friendship didn't start that way . . . It didn't start real."

Worry lines spread across Claudine's face. "What do you mean?"

"I gave you gayuma." I feel an odd sense of relief saying it. Finally, the truth is out. I don't need to keep it any longer. "I gave it to you in Sunday school, a week after you humiliated me in front of everyone. After that . . . you thought you liked me but you really didn't."

"The love potion?" Claudine steps back, horrified. "Why did you do that?"

"I was so mad and hurt and embarrassed and—"

"You were controlling how I felt? What I did?" Claudine

croaks. It looks like she's on the verge of crying. "How could you?"

A lump forms in my throat. "I know. I'm so sorry—"

"All along I thought you were my friend!" Claudine is openly crying now.

"Claudine—"

"STAY AWAY FROM ME!" I try to reach out, but she slaps my hand away. "Don't ever come near me ever again. I don't want to see you. Never, ever!"

Claudine turns on her heel and leaves me by the toilets. Alone.

CHAPTER TWENTY-THREE
Tent Number 283

I sit in our tent, listening to the wind howling around the building. The radio report says the typhoon is stronger than even expected. Isla Pag-Ibig is bracing itself for one of its worst weather events in history.

Which is just great. I have lost my friend, and now I might also lose the new place I call home.

I have only a few hours left to gain Claudine's forgiveness, and I know at this point, there's no chance I'll get it. I can accept my Balik if it comes to it, but I still wish I could make things right with Claudine.

I'm not able to talk to Lolo Sebyo much because tent number 283 has become very busy. So many people need calming potions. But in a brief moment of peace between clients, I ask him how I'll know if I've managed to appease the magic and prevent my Balik.

"You will know when it happens," he says. Lolo Sebyo

gives me a reassuring squeeze. "Your friend will forgive you. I know she will."

I appreciate Lolo's confidence, but I can't say I feel the same. Claudine said she never wants to see me again. Don't I have to respect that? "I'm not sure about that, Lolo—"

Suddenly, cold air envelops our tent. It's so cold that it's as if we're inside a giant freezer.

Kidlat jolts awake from his nap. He stands straight with his ears upright and lets out a low howl.

Lolo Sebyo looks up too, his eyes wide with alarm. "My Bee, didn't you say that you felt true friendship last Saturday evening?"

I bite my lower lip. I *thought* I did.

My heart sinks as I feel the cold, merciless magic of Balik fall on my shoulders like a heavy blanket of darkness. *I made a mistake.*

The gayuma spell broke not in the evening as I thought, but in the afternoon, when Claudine and I spent the day together eating and biking. Even before I realized it, we were already friends. Real friends.

I'm too late asking for her forgiveness. My Balik has come.

Clink! I hear the sound of bottles hitting Lolo Sebyo's cane as he furiously gathers his potions and herbs. He says a prayer as he combines them in a clay pot, then pours the mixture around the tent. The cold air and feeling of darkness leave as suddenly as they arrived.

"That is a circle of protection. It will only last for an hour, but that is enough time for me to brew a potion that will keep your Balik at bay," Lolo explains. "Don't step out of it until I say—"

"Yung bata! Yung bata, nawawala!"

A man shouting about a missing child interrupts Lolo. He comes out of our tent to see what the commotion is all about while I stay inside with Kidlat.

From my vantage point, I see that the shouting man wears the blue shirt of a town official, and he's soliciting people to join them in their search. "There was some kind of argument," he explains. "A young girl was upset and ran out of the evacuation center. Right into the storm."

"Sino yung bata?" Lolo Sebyo asks who the child is.

"The Dimasalang kid."

My heart drops once again. Oh no. Claudine!

CHAPTER TWENTY-FOUR
Scaredy-Cat

"Stay in the tent."

That is the first thing that comes out of Lolo's mouth. I try to argue, but he won't even listen to me.

"I can't brew a potion in this tent." Lolo Sebyo grunts as he drags the wheeled suitcase containing potion ingredients and the clay pot. "The clock is ticking. The longer your Balik is in effect, the harder it will be for me to keep it at bay. You will be in grave danger if I don't. Magic demands retribution, my Bee. Until you render payment, it will not stop haunting you."

"But Claudine—"

"Stay in the tent!" My grandfather leaves before I can say another word.

I ball my fists in frustration. "Argh!"

Don't get me wrong, I love my lolo. I promised him I'll follow his instruction and be more obedient. But I can't sit this one out. I just can't. This is my friend we're talking about.

It's my fault Claudine got so upset. It's also my fault I've gotten Balik. No one is to blame but me, and I have to fix it.

Even if it means stepping out of this magical protective circle.

"Kidlat, stay here." I sound like Lolo, but I can't bring my dog. It's too dangerous. "I'll get Claudine."

I try to pick up Kidlat, but he growls at me.

I don't need to speak dog to know what he's saying. Kidlat wants to come with me, and he's not letting me go until I take him along.

"Argh! You're so frustrating." I put the harness on Kidlat and clip on his leash. "Fine. But stay close to me."

As soon as I step out of the tent, I feel a familiar blast of cold air and darkness looming over me. But I set my fear aside.

This is for Claudine.

I push a bench under the window behind our tent and step on it. I climb out of the window ahead of Kidlat, carefully finding my footing on the ground. I let my eyes adjust to the darkness before hoisting my dog out with me.

The wind is so strong, even the tiny drops of water hitting my face are already painful. I take a deep breath. There is only one place Claudine will attempt to go. That one place she loves and feel safe—the lighthouse of Mount Mahal.

"Okay, good boy. Let's do this. Let's go rescue our friend."

"CLAUDINE! WHERE ARE YOU?"

But no matter how loud I shout, my voice gets muffled by the wind.

The typhoon brought with it an onslaught of torrential rain, making it even harder to see. It's like everything is blanketed with white mist that's really the rain and the wind. Electrical wires, though devoid of power, have been ripped from the posts that hold them.

Suddenly, a piece of metal sheeting, which might have been a part of someone's roofing, flies in front of us and slams into the wall of the building across the street.

I gasp and jump back, my heart racing.

"Stay close to me, Kidlat." I hold the leash of my dog's harness tighter.

Coconut trees are trying to stand their ground. But most trees bend to the angry, powerful wind. I'm afraid Typhoon Totoy will try to take my dog away.

In the distance, I see a flickering dot of light in the dark: the lighthouse. Would Claudine have tried to seek shelter there? I hope it's close by.

I pick an eastward path, the road she'd likely have taken had she been aiming to get to the lighthouse. The volunteers are covering the other side, the one where the center's entrance is.

Kidlat and I turn left. It's impossible to make progress in this storm, and I can barely make out the shape of the road—the heavy rain and the dark clouds are really making it hard for me to see anything clearly.

And that's when we hear a voice. It's muffled, but it gets louder as we move closer and closer to the road. It's hard to see anything, but we keep walking.

"Saklolo! Help! I'm over here."

We finally find Claudine and Winter huddled under a mango tree.

Claudine is shivering. I wish I'd brought a jacket with me.

"My foot hurts!" cries Claudine, holding her left foot with one hand and Winter with the other.

"Let me see." I take Claudine's ankle and lightly press it.

"Ouch!" She winces. "Do you think it's broken?"

I bite my lip. "I don't know. Can you stand?"

Claudine pushes herself against the tree trunk to an upright position. But once she tries to take a step with her left foot, she wails in pain. "It hurts! It hurts so bad!"

I don't know what's wrong with her, but nothing seems to be bleeding or anything horrible like that. One thing is certain—we need to go back and get help for Claudine's injury before it gets worse.

"Hold your cat tight, then put your other arm around me." I grunt when she does. Claudine is heavier than I thought.

It's hard to walk when you have an injured girl with a cat leaning on you for support in the middle of a raging typhoon. It's even harder to walk when you have to weave through a road strewn with fallen trees and debris flying in front of you. Still, we trudge on. And before long, we finally make it across the street.

Then lightning streaks across the sky, followed by the loud boom of thunder.

MEOW! Winter lets out a loud, scared hiss. She scratches Claudine, who drops the cat in pain.

As Winter runs off, Kidlat tugs on his leash hard. I lose my grip, and he follows the cat.

"Kidlat!" I call out to him, but he doesn't stop running until he catches Winter. Thankfully, the cat doesn't get far. Kidlat grabs the skin on the back of Winter's neck with his teeth, the same way tigers and lions carry their young. But the strong winds and the flying debris are making it hard for the animals to make it back to us.

I guide Claudine to the nearest building. There's a mango tree beside it, but it seems to be holding its ground against the wind.

"Stay here," I order Claudine. "I'll get them. Use the wall for support."

Claudine nods. "Be careful!"

I run to Kidlat and Winter as fast as I can, jumping over fallen branches and debris. Kidlat sees me and hurries to where I am while still carrying the struggling cat. I take Winter from Kidlat and hoist her onto my shoulder the way Claudine does. Winter's claws dig into my skin, but I just ignore the pain.

I wind Kidlat's leash around my wrist on my free arm and pick him up. "You're not getting away from me this time, little guy."

The three of us then weave through the debris and falling branches back to Claudine.

Suddenly, a strong gust of wind blows at the mango tree beside Claudine. A branch breaks, falling on the overhang of the building where Claudine is taking shelter.

"WATCH OUT, CLAUDINE!"

Claudine screams as the roof collapses. She tries to run, but she trips and falls. A portion of the roof lands on her injured leg. Claudine groans in pain.

My adrenaline kicks in. Never mind the danger, I need to help her.

I put Kidlat down, but he whines and bites at my shorts. As usual, he realizes what I plan to do. It's like we have our own language without needing to say anything. I just need to feel and think, and he'll feel and know what I felt and thought.

"I have to, good boy. She's my friend," I whisper to his furry ear, handing him Winter. To my relief, he carries her again by the skin on her neck. "Keep that silly cat safe."

My dog whimpers through his mouthful of cat.

It's getting harder and harder to walk in the storm now. Small debris scratch my arm and my face, but never mind that. The magic of Balik can do whatever it wants with me, as long as I save my friend.

I keep pushing the fallen branches and wood and metal sheets from the collapsed roof. I grimace as the metal cuts my hands. Whatever happens, I'm going to save Claudine.

Finally, I reach her.

"You didn't leave me," Claudine sobs. "I thought I was going to die here alone."

"No way." I shake my head. "I'll never, ever leave you. You're my friend. Whether or not you want to be mine."

Claudine smiles weakly.

"Okay, we have to get you out of there," I say, walking to one side of the tree trunk. "When I say go, crawl backward."

Claudine nods tearfully.

"One, two, three— Ahhh!" I lift the heavy roof that's crushing Claudine's foot. "GO!"

Claudine crawls as I instruct.

I drop the roof with a thud.

I've done it!

Just then, I hear something crack. I look up and find a thick, heavy branch falling toward me. I can only stare at it in shock as Claudine screams for me to move.

WAH-ROOF!

Faster than lightning, Kidlat propels his little body forward and pushes me with his front paws.

I fall on the ground, scraping my hands and knees. When I stand and look around, my dog is nowhere in sight. All I can see is the huge branch that was supposed to hit me.

Then, beneath the branch's leaves, I hear the sound of a dog's cry. The sorrowful, sorrowful yelping of a dog in pain.

My dog.

"KIDLAT!"

CHAPTER TWENTY-FIVE
Sagip

Everything that happens next is a blur.

Somehow, the adults found us, and we're now back inside the evacuation center. A volunteer nurse is tending to Claudine's foot outside our family's tent. Mom and Dad are helping Lolo Sebyo find the necessary potions in our luggage to save my dog while I cradle Kidlat in my arms.

"I'm sorry, Jolina," Claudine sobs. "I'm so sorry!"

Claudine tries to enter our tent, but her mother stops her.

"Let's give them space, anak," Tita Peachy says as she ushers her daughter away.

"Please, Lolo, save him," I beg as Lolo Sebyo joins me on the floor and begins his healing prayer. I can feel my dog's labored breathing. It's getting worse every second. "Please save my good boy."

"Give him to me, little Bee." Lolo Sebyo takes Kidlat from me, gently laying him on his side. He pours brown liquid in his hand and rubs his palms together. He spreads more of the oil all over my dog as he continues to pray.

I can't hear what Lolo is saying, but I can feel the increasing urgency in his voice. The happy lines near his eyes turn to worry lines as he prays.

I say a prayer of my own.

Please, Kidlat. Don't leave me.

I love you.

So, so much.

I'd be lost without you.

But Kidlat's breathing continues to slow down. Lolo Sebyo prays even harder.

"He's resisting me," he mutters. Lolo Sebyo lifts Kidlat's paw. "Let me in, little dog. Let my magic heal you."

Kidlat opens an eye, staring at my grandfather.

Lolo Sebyo's lips form a grim line. I can see a look of understanding dawning upon him. He nods. "As you wish."

"What do you mean?" I choke back a sob. "I don't understand! Save him, Lolo!"

Kidlat shifts his gaze to me. He blinks and wags his tail once, too weak to bark or lift his head.

No. You're not saying goodbye. You just can't. I don't know what I'll do if you leave me.

"Bee, you have to let him go."

"I can't. Save him!" I cling on to Kidlat in desperation. *Don't go. You're my best friend. I love you.*

"Kidlat is saving you. Sinasagip ka nya. He wants to save you from something terrible."

"No, Lolo. Save him." Tears flow down my cheeks. It hurts. It hurts so much. *I don't need saving. I just need Kidlat to stay alive.* "Please save him, Lolo! Please!"

"I'm sorry, little Bee. I've tried, but he doesn't want me to."

"You haven't tried hard enough!" I hug Kidlat close to my chest. I can feel his life slipping away. "Don't go. Don't leave me."

"Let him go, little Bee."

Kidlat coughs. His body shudders. The blanket of darkness lifts itself from me, and I feel free.

"No. No. No!" I sob. Every bit of my heart breaks, shattering into a million pieces. Because at that moment, I know he's gone.

My Kidlat is gone.

CHAPTER TWENTY-SIX
Goodbye

This is all my fault. If I hadn't been so selfish and angry and so bent on getting even, Kidlat would still be alive. I made bad choices, and in the end, it's my best friend who took the hit.

And he definitely did.

That giant branch was sent by my Balik to injure me. If I had stayed where I was, I might have survived, but I would have lived with a constant reminder of my mistake. If I've learned anything from the magic of Balik, it is that it's going to punish you for what you did.

But for a small dog like Kidlat, the accident was fatal.

You see, what's worse was that he had a choice. Kidlat could have let Lolo Sebyo's magic heal those internal injuries.

But he didn't.

Kidlat chose to do a Sagip on me. He chose to give up his life so I could live mine peacefully. He didn't have to, but he did.

Until his dying breath, my loyal dog's last act was to selflessly save and protect me, even though I brought this Balik upon myself.

I wish I could turn back time and tell my past self about the terrible cost of the magic of revenge. But I can't.

No amount of magic can turn back time or bring the dead back to life.

Kidlat is gone. My good boy is totally gone.

I'm sorry I took you for granted, my friend.

I'm so sorry I failed you.

You are my everything.

"They have to take him now, Bee," Dad says, gently coaxing Kidlat's lifeless body from me. "You have to let him go."

I let go of Kidlat's body. But I will never, ever let *him* go.

Never.

CHAPTER TWENTY-SEVEN
Seven Candles

It's funny how time passes. When you're too numbed with pain to care, you don't notice time ticking by. I go through each hour like a paper boat floating on Kaibigan River, drifting along wherever the current takes me.

Next thing I know, two days have gone by and it's time for us to return home.

The shelter people took good care of Kidlat's body. They heard what happened, that my good boy was a hero. They treated his remains with the utmost respect. They even said a prayer and held a salute for him when we left the evacuation center with Kidlat's remains and Lolo Sebyo's live chickens.

Our house is a mess. The storm surge flooded the entire first floor, leaving mud and debris and the stench of rotting seaweed. The eatery's food supply and dinnerware are missing, probably washed to sea when the waters receded.

I know Lolo Sebyo and my parents are aching to clean and fix things up, but Kidlat was part of the family. Sending him off comes first.

We bury Kidlat in the backyard.

I stand like a statue beside Lolo Sebyo as Mom and Dad dig a hole under the mango tree. I chose that spot specifically—right above it is the tree branch Kidlat and I loved to spend afternoons on. The mango tree that we believe to be magic, still standing strong even after the typhoon and the storm surge that rushed from the sea.

Maybe the mango tree will also protect Kidlat's final resting place.

"Start lighting the candles, Bee," Mom says as she continues to shovel dirt to cover Kidlat's tiny coffin. Her voice is hoarse, like she's trying not to cry.

I light the candles. There are seven candles in all, one for each of the years he was with me. Seven years—he was with me that long, more than half the time I've lived on this earth.

But I am still here, and Kidlat is not.

I try to cry but can't. I've run out of tears to shed.

Once Mom and Dad are done shoveling back the soil, Lolo Sebyo blesses Kidlat's grave. We say prayers for our beloved dog, standing still as we silently bid him farewell.

Goodbye, my friend. I love you.

Mom and Dad return to cleaning the house. But my grandfather stays with me.

Lolo Sebyo puts an arm around my shoulders. "Don't worry, little Bee. He will return to you. I do not know how and I do not know when, but he will."

"I hope so, Lolo." I let out a long sigh. "I really miss him."

"So do I." Lolo Sebyo releases me and reaches for his cane. "Come, my child. Let us go sit on the bench. I'm afraid my bones are not as strong as they used to be."

"Okay po, Lolo."

The bench outside Lolo Sebyo's lab is right beside Kidlat's grave. I can see the candles flicker from here. The flames continue to burn even as the sea breeze tries to blow them out. The candles are from Lolo's stock, so I'm sure it's because of magic.

"I have been meaning to talk to you, little Bee." Lolo Sebyo leans on his cane, facing me.

I've been waiting for this conversation. After all, Lolo Sebyo was the one who tried to save Kidlat. But there was no privacy in the evacuation center, even with the tent partitions. I'm thankful my grandfather spared me the shame of being overheard.

"That was very brave of you, going after your friend."

I meet his gaze in surprise.

Lolo Sebyo smiles. "There aren't many eleven-year-olds who would walk right into a storm to save their friend. But next time, do as I say. If you're going to be the great arbularyo I know you'll be, you need to learn to follow my instructions."

"Yes po, Lolo, I promise."

"Remember, righting a wrong with another wrong does not make it right." Lolo Sebyo shakes loose soil off his cane. "Being an arbularyo is a huge responsibility, and magic should not be taken lightly."

"Opo. I know that now po." I hang my head in shame.

"I am certain you have learned your lesson." My grandfather strokes my hair. "The brave little one saved you from what could have been a very challenging future. He wanted you to have a second chance in life—to live a life untainted with Balik. It is a chance for you to be happy again. All because he loved you."

I've always taken magic for granted—like, I deserved it because it was my birthright. I expected the magic to yield to me, and I couldn't see that it was a force beyond my control—a force that I *shouldn't* even try to control. Maybe that's why I've been so terrible at it and only succeeded when I was overwhelmed with anger and hurt. But I think I'm beginning to understand it now.

I can't use magic for selfish reasons, expecting no consequences just because I make myself believe that what I'm doing is right. What's wrong is wrong. Taking control of someone and playing with their emotions is definitely wrong.

"I messed up real bad, Lolo. Maybe I don't deserve to be an arbularyo like you."

"We all make mistakes, my Bee." Lolo Sebyo cups my

chin and gently turns my head to face him. "But you have been given another chance. That is a privilege. Not everyone gets the same chance as you. Do not waste it."

"I won't. Promise po."

A man clears his throat. We look up to the direction of the sound, finding Dad in the yard once again. "I'm sorry to interrupt, but there are people here to see you."

Lolo Sebyo stands. "Lead the way, Rainier."

But Dad shakes his head. "No, Papa. They're here for Jolina."

Dad steps aside to reveal Tita Peachy, Tita Raven, Winter, and my former BFFAE, in crutches and with a bandaged foot.

"Hi," says Claudine.

CHAPTER TWENTY-EIGHT
Promise to a Friend

As expected, Mom turns into an anxious mess upon seeing her bosses. She drops her broom and dust pan and hurries to join us.

"Ma'am Peachy, Ma'am Raven!" she gasps. Her disheveled hair has dry leaves in it, and her face is streaked with mud. "What can I get you? Water? Juice?"

"We're fine," Tita Peachy says. "Don't stress yourself, Sunshine. You have enough to worry about already. We were wondering if you needed a ride home, but they said you'd left the shelter already. But we needed to see your family, especially this girl." Tita Peachy takes my hands and covers them with her own. "Jolina. Maraming, maraming salamat. Thank you so, so much. You saved my baby."

I look up and find Mom, Dad, and Lolo Sebyo beaming with pride. I turn away. I don't deserve this recognition after what I did.

"She would have done the same for me."

We may not be friends anymore, but from the short time I've known Claudine, I know she wouldn't have hesitated to save me if I needed it too.

"She's a great girl. We'd be so lost without her." Tita Raven smiles. She tilts her head in Mom's direction. "Sunshine, a word? There are some things I would like to discuss with you. Our resort manager has decided to move back to her family in Leyte. Peachy and I believe you would be perfect for the position."

"Oh my!" Mom wipes her dirty hands on her apron. "Yes. Yes, of course, ma'am. Thank you so much!"

"I don't want the family of my daughter's rescuer to have a difficult time rising from this terrible typhoon." Tita Peachy smiles at me one more time. "The storm surge may have flooded it, but I will help you rebuild Bagayan Food Haus. And maybe even expand it! Raven and I have always wanted to source some of our hotel's food service needs."

As soon as the adults leave, Claudine sets Winter on the ground. The cat walks to where Kidlat is buried and meows in sorrow.

I feel a knot form in my throat again.

"We brought flowers for Kidlat." Claudine wipes away a tear. "Is that where he's buried?"

"Yeah." I step aside to let Claudine through.

She lays a bouquet of mums and yellow roses on Kidlat's grave.

"He was a good boy."

"I miss him so much." I wipe away a tear that has fallen down my cheek. "I also missed you."

Claudine bites her lower lip. "That wasn't very nice, you giving me gayuma."

"I'm sorry." The floodgates open, and I'm crying again. "I think about it all the time. I had no right to control your emotions and thoughts like that. I'm so, so sorry. One day, sana mapatawad mo ko. I hope you can forgive me one day."

"I do already. Don't you feel it? I know why you did it. I was terrible. I kept saying we just got off on the wrong foot, but it was me trying to make myself feel better. I made you feel unwelcome. I bullied you. It's no excuse, but I was really jealous of you—a cool Manilenya with a wonderful family. But you forgave me and I thought all was good. I felt so betrayed when you said you used a gayuma on me. I didn't know what had been real and what hadn't."

"I know. I'm sorry—"

"Hey, hey. Didn't I say I forgive you already? I'm hurt you did it, but I understand. What I'm trying to say is . . ." Claudine takes my hand. "I've already forgiven you."

I throw my arms around Claudine and hug her tight. "You're so kind."

"It's really hard not to forgive the person who saved my life." She gently extricates herself from me, smiling. She flips her hair in usual Claudine fashion. "And Winter's. It's because of you and Kidlat that we're here."

I hug her once more. "Do you think it's possible for us to be friends again?"

"I guess," she says, shrugging. Then she narrows her eyes. "It's going to be a while before I trust your cooking again though."

I grin. "You can watch me cook."

Claudine grins back. "Cool."

"Did you really lock yourself and Winter in your bedroom?"

"Yeah. That's actually what I wanted to tell you before you sprung that whole 'I gave you gayuma' thing on me," says Claudine, smirking. "I wasn't planning on staying inside too long. My food supply would only last me until the evening. Can't live on potato chips and chocolate milk forever."

"True." I nod in mock seriousness. "You'd get a tummy ache. And poop all day!"

Claudine and I burst out laughing. We laugh until our insides hurt.

It's so nice to laugh with a friend again. *My* friend.

As our laughter dies down, Claudine clears her throat. "One more thing."

"Yes?"

"I just thought you should know . . . You didn't have to give me gayuma. I always wanted us to be friends." Claudine glances at Kidlat's grave. "I think Kidlat did too. He was always nice to me."

"Yeah." I agree. My dog knew many things. "He was the best dog ever."

Claudine puts an arm around me. "I'm glad we're friends again."

I lean my head on Claudine's shoulder, looking up at the now-clear blue sky. "So am I."

CHAPTER TWENTY-NINE

The Twenty-Fifth of April

Today is the twenty-fifth of April, the day I was born. The day I turn twelve.

When Kidlat was still alive, I would wake up on my birthday mornings to find him sitting by my pillow with a gift. They were mostly sticks, rocks, or random things like a plastic cup or an old toothbrush.

I've kept all his gifts in a box. Though it breaks my heart knowing that I'll never add another trinket to it, I feel blessed I have a box like this at all. Kidlat was truly an amazing dog.

"J-Bee! Hurry up. The boat is waiting," Mom calls from downstairs.

"Coming!" I close the box and hide it under my bed. On my way to the door, I take a packed duffel bag and hoist it onto my shoulder.

Kidlat has been gone for less than a year. It feels like

forever. Everything is so different and familiar at the same time. I can't say that I'm over it—I don't think I ever will be. Losing my beloved dog is like a wound that has scabbed over but continues to throb underneath.

"Ready?" Mom takes my bag when I meet her at the foot of the stairs. I nod, and we head down to the beach through the backyard.

If Kidlat were alive, he would be weirded out by how different our beach now looks. There are fewer grown trees, but there are lots of young ones we planted a few months back. Fallen logs are turned into makeshift benches where more residents—not just me—spend time on them, thinking about what they've lost and what the future may be.

"Hey, birthday girl! Get your butt in here," Claudine calls from the boat my family rented, where Dad and the boat crew of two are loading the coolers and picnic stuff.

Like most outrigger boats used for tourism, this boat has a covered passenger area. And in that area with Claudine are Lolo Sebyo and my friends who'll be celebrating my birthday with me on the mainland—Angelou, Marvin, Bobby, Judy, and Ann.

We're midway down the beach when Mom suddenly stops. She blurts out a string of bad words. "I totally forgot the balut!"

"Where is it?"

"On the bench beside Lolo's lab."

"Okay. I'll get it," I volunteer. We can't have a picnic

without balut. It's my favorite and was Kidlat's. It wouldn't be right not having it as part of a meal celebrating my special day.

"Thanks, sweetheart." Mom throws me a grateful look as she gathers our stuff. "Be quick, okay?"

The basket of balut is exactly where Mom says it is—the bench beside the place where we laid Kidlat to rest. Before leaving, I take a flower from the hibiscus shrub we planted between the lab and the mango tree.

I place the flower on Kidlat's grave. "I miss you, little guy."

He would have loved our adventure for the day.

My family and friends are waiting, so I hurry back to the boat. Just last year, on this same day, I was saying goodbye to my old home in Marikina. This year, I'm celebrating my twelfth birthday in my new home with my new forever friends.

As my sandaled feet touch the warm seawater, I hear another familiar sound behind me.

WOOF!

A puppy emerges from behind the coconut trees. It has white-and-black markings on its brown fur. The dog bounds down the beach and heads straight for me.

"Bee! Get in the boat now!" Mom shrieks. There's a huge splash as she jumps off the boat and wades toward me. "Shoo, dog! Don't hurt my baby."

"It's okay, Mom! It's just a puppy." I don't know why, but I just *know* this dog doesn't mean me any harm. I bring out a cooked fertilized duck egg from my basket. "Do you want a balut, fur-boy? You're a boy, aren't you?"

WOOF! The puppy wags its tail.

But as the dog moves closer, I notice he isn't a boy after all.

"Oh, it's a pretty girl," Mom says, splashing beside me. "Careful, Bee. She might bite you."

"Okay, *girl*, here's a balut." I walk closer to the shore, holding out the egg in my hand. "Do you like balut?"

The dog wolfs down the balut in seconds. She barks happily, going in circles, just like Kidlat used to do when he was excited.

I crouch low to wash my hands.

"JOLINA!" Mom tries to grab me by the shoulders, but the dog's faster. She goes straight for my face . . . and licks my cheek.

"Oh!" I smile, gently pushing her off. I can hear Mom's loud sigh of relief from behind me. "You're welcome."

The dog stares into my eyes. In that moment, I realize what people mean in Mom's telenovelas when they say that the eyes are the windows to one's soul. I glimpse into the dog's soul, and I see someone very, very familiar.

"Mom, I think this dog is—" Water splashes on my face as the dog bounds for our boat. She's so bouncy, it's like she has balls on her paws.

"Welcome, you brave good boy," Lolo Sebyo tells the dog as she jumps into the boat.

"I guess this means we're getting a new dog," Mom says. She hands the balut basket to Claudine and guides me through the wooden plank leading up to the boat. Dad helps her get on. "She's a girl, Papa."

"I know." Lolo Sebyo smiles. "Perhaps I should say, 'Welcome back.'"

Marvin frowns. "I don't get it."

"I do," Claudine says, giving my hand a squeeze. I squeeze her hand back.

Lolo Sebyo continues to smile, quietly watching Dad and the crew pull the plank into the boat.

I know what Lolo Sebyo means, but I don't dare hope. What if we're both wrong? I don't want to break my heart all over again.

"I'm calling you Magiting," I tell the dog. Names have meaning, and this name is perfect for her. "It means 'courageous,' you know."

"He's cute," Angelou says.

"Be careful. It might have rabies." Judy grabs her sister's hand. "Don't touch it, Ann. And keep your cat away from it, Claudine. It might attack."

"This fur-baby won't hurt Winter," Claudine assures the girl. She gives me a smile. "Magiting is her friend."

Sure enough, Winter lets out a loud meow. She jumps off Claudine's lap and rubs her body against the dog. Magiting gives Winter a kiss.

"I think she's okay." Bobby peers closer at the dog.

"Her ears are marked. That means she's been spayed and vaccinated by the government. She's probably one of the animal shelter dogs who escaped during Typhoon Totoy."

"Welcome to the family, Magiting," Dad says. He hands a long bamboo pole to the boatman, who begins pushing the boat away from the shore. "We'll need to let the shelter know we found her, but I'm sure they'll let us adopt her officially."

The boat's motor starts. It's so loud, it drowns any conversation in the boat. Isla Pag-Ibig grows smaller and smaller the farther we go.

Mom is leaning on Dad, their eyes fixed on the view of the sea. Lolo Sebyo and all my friends save for Claudine are sound asleep and doing a snoring orchestra.

I look at the dog between Claudine and me.

"It's him, isn't it, J-Bee?" Claudine whispers in my ear. "It really is him."

"Yes, it is," I say, smiling through my tears. Claudine gives my hand another squeeze.

The puppy moves to my other side, the one nearer to the edge of the boat. She closes her eyes and feels the breeze on her face.

I have my whole life to look forward to now because of this very good, very brave dog.

"You came back for me." A tear falls down my check as I pat Magiting's head. "I didn't think you would, but you did. I love you, Kidlat . . . or should I say, Magiting."

Woof!

Jolina's Yema Balls Recipe

Do you want to know how to make the yema balls Claudine loves so much? Well, you're in luck! I'm going to share with you the super-secret recipe of Bagayan Food Haus's famous yema balls.

Before you begin cooking, be sure to ask an adult to supervise you in the kitchen. I cooked yema balls without my parents or Lolo Sebyo knowing—you've seen what happened to me. It's a recipe for total disaster (pun intended) if you don't have adult supervision. I'm pretty sure you're not putting gayuma in your candies, but you never know what bad things might happen. It's better to be safe than sorry.

Remember: Safety first! Always have an adult supervise when you use the stove or sharp implements.

Ingredients:

4 egg yolks

4 medium-sized calamansi (Philippine lime), each cut in half. If you can't find calamansi, you can substitute it with 3 tablespoons lemon juice and 1 tablespoon fresh orange juice.

1 300-ml (10 oz.) can condensed milk

2 tablespoons salted butter, plus half a teaspoon for greasing

Granulated white sugar for coating

Candy wrapper of your choice, or food-grade cellophane wrap, cut into 10–20 3-inch squares

Yields: 20–30 yema balls, depending on how big or small you roll them.

Directions:

1. Grease a plate with butter and set aside.
2. Separate the yolks from the egg whites and place them into a bowl. My dad has this cool technique of simply cracking the shell in two and letting the egg white drip into a bowl. But he's a seasoned

cook, so you might want to use an egg separator instead. Or, even better, ask your parent or guardian to do it for you!

3. Squeeze the halved calamansi (or squeeze the lemons and add orange juice) into a small bowl. Make sure that the juice is free of seeds. There's nothing worse than biting into a stray bitter seed when eating yema balls. It just totally ruins the candy. Take note though—a calamansi may be very small, but it sure packs a punch! It is very tart.

4. Mix the egg yolks, calamansi juice, and can of condensed milk in a nonstick 8-inch pan.

5. Once you're sure the ingredients are evenly mixed, it's time to turn on the flame! Remember that adult supervision is required when preparing to use the stove. Cook the mixture over very low heat, stirring constantly.

6. Keep stirring until the mixture starts to thicken. Add the butter.

7. Turn off the heat once the mixture gets to a taffy-like consistency and separates from the pan. Overcooking will give you hard yema balls—and we don't want that.

8. Using a spatula, transfer the mixture to the plate greased with butter. Let the yema cool down enough for you to handle.

9. Scoop your preferred amount of yema and roll the

candy into balls. The smaller the ball, the more yema balls you'll have!

10. Roll the balls in white sugar, then wrap them individually with your candy wrappers.

If you live in a temperate country, the yema balls can last up to 4 weeks at room temperature. But if you live in a tropical country like the Philippines, where it can get really hot, it's best to store them in the fridge. Refrigerated yema can last up to 7 weeks. Yema balls are such a very tasty sweet treat though, so it's very possible there won't be any left to store. Enjoy!

Author's Note

This book was very difficult to write. It was probably one of the hardest—if not *the* hardest—work I have written to date.

In the past thirty-eight years (that's a lot of years), I have lost a number of pets. But none of them were as painful as losing my dog, Kubrick, in 2016. He was a smart little guy. So smart, in fact, that he was able to do agility training with me.

This was a big deal. To be successful, a dog and their human partner need to have a special kind of bond—a bond that will let you give commands without speaking them out loud. Like, your dog will know what to do by looking at and feeling you. Just like Kidlat knowing what Jolina is thinking and feeling without them speaking the same language.

Kubrick and I had that kind of bond. Then he got sick, and I lost him.

I couldn't really bring myself to commemorate him until now, with this book. It took me a long time to muster the courage to write about him and to confront my feelings. And that's totally okay.

If you've lost a pet, like Jolina and me, there are times

when it may seem as if you're alone in your grief—like people just don't understand.

I get you. Losing a pet is one of the hardest things a human has to go through.

Take all the time you need to process your feelings. Remember: Somewhere out there, your pet is watching over you.

Real-life Sagip Stories

Sagip is a common belief in the Philippines. It literally translates to "save" and happens when an animal—most often a beloved pet—sacrifices their life to save a person from illness or bad luck. The logical part of me thinks that Sagip is our way of making sense of a pet's death. But a part of me believes it's real.

In her opinion editorial, "Saved by the Dog," Alya B. Honasan talks about being saved by Larry, her twelve-year-old black Labrador retriever, from a heart ailment.[1] She was at risk of cardiomyopathy when Larry got sick suddenly. Larry pulled through, but Alya was shocked at the vet's findings: Larry had cardiomyopathy.

A similar thing had happened to my friend Aileen Apolo-de Jesus. Her beloved dog, Jolly, passed away at the same time that Aileen had heart surgery.

My dog Kubrick saved me so many times. Once, I had a really bad flu. My illness suddenly disappeared right before I went to the doctor. That same day, Kubrick got a fever out of the blue. The vet couldn't find anything wrong with him. Like in Alya's story about Larry, our vet asked if anyone was sick in our family. I said that I had been. She smiled and told me I was lucky to have a loyal dog like Kubrick.

Maybe it was just a coincidence. Maybe I was only imagining things. But I will always believe my loyal dog saved me from something horrible when he passed away. It was just something he would do.

Like Jolina says in the story, everyday miracles are a form of magic. Kubrick was my miracle, and so is every pet we have in our lives.

A Culture of Respecting Elders

Aside from believing in miracles, treating elders with respect is also very important to Filipinos. The "mano" gesture that Jolina makes is a greeting and a way to request blessing from someone older. She also uses "po" and "opo" frequently when talking to her elders. These words of respect are distinctly Filipino and don't have a direct translation in English, but they add formality and respect.

Bullying and Getting Bullied

Respecting our elders doesn't mean we can't talk to them openly. If you or someone you know is being bullied, it's very important that you tell an adult you trust about it. Everyone has the right to feel safe from bullying—and that includes you. You shouldn't have to go through it alone. Ask for help as soon as you can.

On Being "Poor"

When I was in middle school, I never felt like I totally fit in. You see, my family was of a lower-middle income class; our family's combined monthly income fell between ₱23,381 to ₱46,761.[2] Using today's exchange rate, that would be about US $465.20 to US $930.38 per month for our then-family of four.[3] But I studied at a private school where most of my classmates were well-off. My parents worked really hard to put me through school, but when it got really tough, my grandmother helped us.

Some of my meaner classmates made it perfectly clear to me that I didn't belong. This made me feel ashamed. I made excuses for why I couldn't join certain field trips. I removed the labels from my clothes so they wouldn't see that my family could only afford cheap brands. I lied about having a designer dress when it was really my creative mom who had made it.

Then I met people who became my closest friends. They didn't care that I was poor. They stood by me, and I learned to hold my head high.

Not everyone will be born with privilege. You shouldn't let your circumstances define you. Rich or poor, you're you. Be proud of who you are.

Pag-Ibig Island

Let me spare you the trouble of trying to find Pag-Ibig Island: It doesn't exist. ☺ But it was based on places I've visited outside Metro Manila in the Philippines. Most of Pag-Ibig Island's geography was inspired by the charming town of Bulusan in Bicol.

1. Alya B. Honasan, "Saved by the Dog," *Lifestyle.INQ*, Philippines, Philippine Daily Inquirer, 31 October 2013, page 1, lifestyle.inquirer.net/134055/saved-by -the-dog/, (accessed 7 June 2020).

2. Sandra Zialcita, "EXPLAINER: Who Are the Filipino Middle Class?" *CNN Philippines*, Philippines, Nine Media Corp., 25 April 2020, page 1, cnnphilippines .com/news/2020/4/25/explainer-who-are-the-Filipino-middle-class.html, (accessed 7 June 2020).

3. Bloomberg, US Dollar - *Philippine Peso Exchange Rate* [website], bloomberg .com/quote/USDPHP:CUR, (accessed 16 June 2020).

Acknowledgments

How do you say "thank you" multiple times without saying the same thing over and over again? It's a challenge that's worth every single word and character—this book wouldn't be a book without the wonderful people who helped me make it happen.

First off, many thanks to justwanderingtours.com for giving me and my husband the best Bulusan experience. Our stay in the province was so memorable, I decided to base my fictional island on it. Thank you for your hospitality and spectacular service.

My deepest thanks to my champion and agent, Alyssa Eisner Henkin. Thank you for always believing in me and my work. Sometimes I still find it hard to believe that I'm on my second book already, but here we are! Without you, none of this would have been possible.

I'm eternally grateful to my editor, Emily Seife, who continuously makes me a better writer. Your editorial touch is truly magical. I didn't even need to use a potion to turn my ugly first draft into a decent, publishable manuscript!

To my Scholastic family—thank you for bringing Jolina's story out in the world. Special thanks to Orlando Dos Reis for adopting me (it was so great working with you even for a short time). To production editor Josh Berlowitz, for once again taking good care of my words. To Abigail L. Dela Cruz, for the gorgeous cover I can't stop gushing about! To Baily Crawford, for the beautiful book design, as usual. To Danielle Yadao and Lizette Serrano, for marketing my books so tirelessly and for giving me authorly opportunities that I never thought I'd have.

To my regional Scholastic team in Asia and the Philippines— you have my utmost gratitude. Nurhannis Hisham, Joyce Bautista, Van Patricia B. Ravinera-Abrogena, and Melissa Socorro, thank you for making sure Filipino kids get to read my stories.

My sincere thanks to Kate Heceta, Cara Sobrepeña, and Shealea Iral for your hard work in advocating for marginalized authors. I will forever be grateful for your support and help in getting the word out about my books. You three are the absolute rock stars of book blogging!

So much thanks to Daka Hermon, Hanna Alkaf, Remy Lai, and Elsie Chapman—you make the solo art of writing less lonely. Same goes for my Philippine squad—Rin Chupeco, Tarie Sabido, Hazel Ureta, and Kara Bodegon. Thank you for your friendship and solidarity.

To Isabelle Adrid and Rae Somer—I'd be lost without you two. Thanks for sticking with me.

I'm so grateful for my parents, August and Jocelyn, and my younger sister, Joyce. Not everyone can say they have family as supportive and caring as you. But I can, and I'll always be thankful for that.

To my husband and my best friend, Marc—thank you for being my constant. I will never stop thanking God for having you in my life. I love you, forever and always.

About the Author

Gail D. Villanueva is a Filipino author born and based in the Philippines. *My Fate According to the Butterfly*, her debut novel, was a 2019 Kirkus Best Book of the Year and an NCSS-CBC Notable Social Studies Trade Book for Young People. She's also a web designer, an entrepreneur, and a graphic artist. She loves pineapple pizza, seafood, and chocolate, but not in a single dish together (ewww). Gail and her husband live in the outskirts of Manila with their dogs, ducks, turtles, cats, and one friendly but lonesome chicken. Learn more at gaildvillanueva.com.